CW00501858

Arnold Bennett

The Title

outlook

Arnold Bennett

The Title

1st Edition | ISBN: 978-3-73409-449-1

Place of Publication: Frankfurt am Main, Germany

Year of Publication: 2019

Outlook Verlag GmbH, Germany.

The Title

A COMEDY IN THREE ACTS

BY

ARNOLD BENNETT

LONDON
CHATTO & WINDUS
MCMXVIII

CHARACTERS

MR. CULVER
MRS. CULVER
HILDEGARDE CULVER } theirchildren
JOHN CULVER   }
TRANTO
MISS STARKEY
SAMPSON STRAIGHT
PARLOURMAID

ACT I

An evening between Christmas and New Year, before dinner.

ACT II

The next evening, after dinner.

ACT III

The next day, before lunch.

The scene throughout is a sitting-room in the well-furnished West End abode of the Culvers. There is a door, back. There is also another door (L) leading to Mrs. Culver's boudoir and elsewhere.

ACT I

ACT I

Hildegarde *is sitting at a desk, writing* . John, *in a lounging attitude, is reading a newspaper* .

Enter Tranto, *back* .

TRANTO. Good evening.

HILDEGARDE (*turning slightly in her seat and giving him her left hand, the right still holding a pen*). Good evening. Excuse me one moment.

TRANTO. All right about my dining here to-night? (Hildegarde *nods* .) Larder equal to the strain?

HILDEGARDE. Macaroni.

TRANTO. Splendid.

HILDEGARDE. Beefsteak.

TRANTO. Great heavens! (*imitates sketchily the motions of cutting up a piece of steak. Shaking hands with* John, *who has risen*). Well, John. How are things? Don't let me disturb you. Have a cigarette.

JOHN (*flattered*). Thanks. (*As they light cigarettes* .) You're the first person here that's treated me like a human being.

TRANTO. Oh!

JOHN. Yes. They all treat me as if I was a schoolboy home for the hols.

TRANTO. But you are, aren't you?

JOHN. In a way, of course. But—well, don't you see what I mean?

TRANTO (*sympathetically*). You mean that a schoolboy home for the hols isn't necessarily something escaped out of the Zoo.

JOHN (*warming*). That's it.

TRANTO. In fact, what you mean is you're really an individual very like the rest of us, subject, if I may say so, to the common desires, weaknesses and prejudices of humanity—and not a damned freak.

JOHN (*brightly*). That's rather good, that is. If it's a question of the Zoo, what I say is—what price home? Now, homes *are* extraordinary if you like—I don't know whether you've ever noticed it. School—you can understand

4

school. But home—! Strange things happen here while I'm away.

TRANTO. Yes?

JOHN. It was while I was away they appointed Dad a controller. When I heard—I laughed. Dad a controller! Why, he can't even control mother.

HILDEGARDE (*without looking round*). Oh yes he can.

JOHN (*pretending to start back*). Stay me with flagons! (*Resuming to* Tranto.) And *you're* something new here since the summer holidays.

TRANTO. I never looked at myself in that light. But I suppose I *am* rather new here.

JOHN. Not quite new. But you've made a lot of progress during the last term.

TRANTO. That's comforting.

JOHN. You understand what I mean. You were rather stiff and prim in August —now you aren't a bit.

TRANTO. Just so. Well, I won't ask you what you think of *me* , John—you might tell me—but what do you think of my newspaper?

JOHN. *The Echo* ? I don't know what to think. You see, we don't read newspapers much at school. Some of the masters do. And a few chaps in the Fifth—swank, of course. But speaking generally we don't. Prefects don't. No time.

TRANTO. How strange! Aren't you interested in the war?

JOHN. Interested in the war! Would you mind if I spoke plainly?

TRANTO. I should love it.

JOHN. Each time I come home I wonder more and more whether you people in London have got the slightest notion what war really is. Fact! At school, it's just because we *are* interested in the war that we've no time for newspapers.

TRANTO. How's that?

JOHN. How's that? Well, munition workshops—with government inspectors tumbling all over us about once a week. O.T.C. work. Field days. Cramming fellows for Sandhurst. Not to mention female masters. 'Mistresses,' I ought to say, perhaps. All these things take time.

TRANTO. I never thought of that.

JOHN. No. People don't. However, I've decided to read newspapers in future —it'll be part of my scheme. That's why I was reading *The Echo* . Now, I should like to ask you something about this paper of yours.

TRANTO. Yes.

JOHN. Why do you let Hilda write those articles for you about food economy stunts in the household?

TRANTO. Well—(*hesitating*)

JOHN. Now, I look at things practically. When Hilda'd spent all her dress allowance and got into debt besides, about a year and a half ago, she suddenly remembered she wasn't doing much to help the war, and so she went into the Food Ministry as a typist at thirty-five shillings a week. Next she learnt typing. Then she became an authority on everything. And now she's concocting these food articles for you. Believe me, the girl knows nothing whatever about cookery. She couldn't fry a sausage for nuts. Once the mater insisted on her doing the housekeeping—in the holidays, too! Stay me with flagons!

HILDEGARDE (*without looking round*). Stay you with chocolates, you mean, Johnnie, dear.

JOHN. There you are! Her thoughts fly instantly to chocolates—and in the fourth year of the greatest war that the world—

HILDEGARDE. Etcetera, etcetera.

TRANTO. Then do I gather that you don't entirely approve of your sister's articles?

JOHN. Tripe, I think. My fag could write better. I'll tell you what I do approve of. I approve of that article to-day by that chap Sampson Straight about titles and the shameful traffic in honours, and the rot of the hereditary principle, and all that sort of thing.

TRANTO. I'm glad. Delivers the goods, doesn't he, Mr. Sampson Straight?

JOHN. Well, *I* think so. Who is he?

TRANTO. One of my discoveries, John. He sent me in an article about—let me see, when was it?—about eight months ago. I at once perceived that in Mr. Sampson Straight I had got on to a bit of all right. And I was not mistaken. He has given London beans pretty regularly once a week ever since.

JOHN. He must have given the War Cabinet neuralgia this afternoon, anyhow. I should like to meet him.

TRANTO. I'm afraid that's impossible.

JOHN. Is it? Why?

TRANTO. Well, I haven't met him myself yet. He lives at a quiet country place in Cornwall. Hermit, I believe. Hates any kind of publicity. Absolutely refuses to be photographed.

JOHN. Photographed! I should think not! But couldn't you get him to come and lecture at school? We have frightful swells, you know.

TRANTO. I expect you do. But he wouldn't come.

JOHN. I wish he would. We had a debate the other Saturday night on, Should the hereditary principle be abolished?

TRANTO. And did you abolish it?

JOHN. Did we abolish it? I should say we did. Eighty-five to twenty-one. Some debate, believe *me* !

HILDEGARDE (*looking round*). Yes, but didn't you tell us once that in your Debating Society the speakers always tossed for sides beforehand?

JOHN (*shrugging his shoulders. More confidentially to* Tranto). As I was saying, I'm going to read the papers in future, as part of my scheme. And d'you know what the scheme is? (*Impressively* .) I've decided to take up a political career.

TRANTO. Good!

JOHN. Yes, it was during that hereditary principle debate that I decided. It came over me all of a sudden while I was on the last lap of my speech and the fellows were cheering. And so I want to understand first of all the newspaper situation in London. There are one or two things about it I *don't* understand.

TRANTO. Not more? I can explain the newspaper situation to you in ten words. You know I've got a lot of uncles. I daresay I've got more uncles than anybody else in 'Who's Who.' Well, I own *The Echo* ,—inherited it from my father. My uncles own all the rest of the press—(*airily*) with a few trifling exceptions. That's the London newspaper situation. Quite simple, isn't it?

JOHN. But of course *The Echo* is up against all your uncles' papers—at least it seems so.

TRANTO. Absolutely up against them. Tooth and nail. Daggers drawn. No quarter. Death or victory.

JOHN. But do you and your uncles speak to each other?

TRANTO. Best of friends.

JOHN. But aren't two of your uncles lords?

TRANTO. Yes. Uncle Joe was made an earl not long since—you may have heard of the fuss about it. Uncle Sam's only a miserable baron yet. And Uncle Cuthbert is that paltry insect—a baronet.

JOHN. What did they get their titles for?

TRANTO. Ask me another.

JOHN. Of course I don't want to be personal, but *how* did they get them? Did they—er—buy them?

TRANTO. Don't know.

JOHN. Haven't you ever asked them?

TRANTO. Well, John, you've got relatives yourself, and you probably know there are some things that even the most affectionate relatives *don't* ask each other.

HILDEGARDE (*rising from the desk and looking at John's feet*). Yes, indeed! This very morning I unwisely asked Johnnie whether his socks ever talked. Altercation followed. 'Some debate, believe *me* !'

JOHN (*rising; with scornful tranquillity*). I'd better get ready for dinner. Besides, you two would doubtless like to be alone together for a few precious moments.

HILDEGARDE (*sharply and self-consciously*). What do you mean?

JOHN (*lightly*). Nothing. I thought editor and contributor—

HILDEGARDE. Oh! I see.

JOHN (*stopping at door, and turning round*). Do you mean to say your uncles won't be frightfully angry at Mr. Sampson Straight's articles? Why, dash it, when he's talking about traffic in honours, if he doesn't mean them who does he mean?

TRANTO. My dear friend, stuff like that's meat and drink to my uncles. They put it down like chocolates.

JOHN. Well my deliberate opinion is—it's a jolly strange world. (*Exit quickly, back)* .

TRANTO (*looking at* Hildegarde). So it is. Philosopher, John! Questions rather pointed perhaps; but result in the discovery of new truths. By the way, have I come too early?

HILDEGARDE (*archly)* . How could you? But father's controlling the country half an hour more than usual this evening, and I expect mamma was so angry about it she forgot to telephone you that dinner's moved accordingly. (*With piquancy and humour* .) I was rather surprised to hear when I got home

8

from my Ministry that you'd sent word you'd like to dine to-night.

TRANTO. Were you? Why?

HILDEGARDE. Because last week when mamma *asked* you for to-night, you said you had another engagement.

TRANTO. Oh! I'd forgotten I'd told her that. Still, I really had another engagement.

HILDEGARDE. The Countess of Blackfriars—you said.

TRANTO. Yes. Auntie Joe's. I've just sent her a telephone message to say I'm ill and confined to the house.

HILDEGARDE. Which house?

TRANTO. I didn't specify any particular house.

HILDEGARDE. And are you ill?

TRANTO. I am not…. To get back to the realm of fact, when I read Sampson Straight's article about the degradation of honours this afternoon—

HILDEGARDE. Didn't you read it before you published it?

TRANTO. No. I had to rush off and confront the Medical Board at 9 a.m. I felt certain the article would be all right.

HILDEGARDE. And it wasn't all right.

TRANTO (*positively*). Perfectly all right.

HILDEGARDE. You don't seem quite sure. Are we still in the realm of fact, or are we slipping over the frontier?

TRANTO. The article was perfectly all right. It rattled off from beginning to end like a machine-gun, and must have caused enormous casualties. Only I thought Auntie Joe might be one of the casualties. I thought it might put her out of action as a hostess for a week or so. You see, for me to publish such an onslaught on new titles in the afternoon, and then attempt to dine with the latest countess the same night—and she my own aunt—well, it might be regarded as a bit—thick. So I'm confined to the house—this house as it happens.

HILDEGARDE. But you told John your people would take the article like meat and drink.

TRANTO. What if I did? John can't expect to discover the whole truth about everything at one go. He's found out it's a jolly strange world. That ought to satisfy him for to-day. Besides, he only asked me about my uncles. He said nothing about my uncles' wives. You know what women are—I mean wives.

HILDEGARDE. Oh, I do! Mother is a marvellous specimen.

TRANTO. I haven't told you the worst.

HILDEGARDE. I hope no man everwill.

TRANTO. The worst is this. Auntie Joe actually thinks *I* 'm Sampson Straight.

HILDEGARDE. She doesn't!

TRANTO. She does. She has an infinite capacity for belief. The psychology of the thing is as follows. My governor died a comparatively poor man. A couple of hundred thousand pounds, more or less. Whereas Uncle Joe is worth five millions—and Uncle Joe was going to adopt me, when Auntie Joe butted in and married him. She used to arrange the flowers for his first wife. Then she arranged *his* flowers. Then she became a flower herself and he had to gather her. Then she had twins, and my chances of inheriting that five millions (*he imitates the noise of a slight explosion*) short-circuited! Well, I didn't care a volt—not a volt! I've got lots of uncles left who are quite capable of adopting me. But I didn't really want to be adopted at all. To adopt me was only part of Uncle Joe's political game. It was my *Echo* that he was after adopting. But I'd sooner run my *Echo* on my own than inherit Uncle Joe's controlling share in twenty-five daily papers, seventy-one weekly papers, six monthly magazines, and three independent advertising agencies. I know I'm a poor man, but I'm quite ready to go on facing the world bravely with my modest capital of a couple of hundred thousand pounds. Only Auntie Joe can't understand that. She's absolutely convinced that I have a terrific grudge against her and her twins, and that in order to gratify that grudge I myself personally write articles against all her most sacred ideals under the pseudonym of Sampson Straight. I've pointed out to her that I'm a newspaper proprietor, and no newspaper proprietor ever *could* write. No use! She won't listen.

HILDEGARDE. Then she thinks you're a liar.

TRANTO. Oh, not at all. Only a journalist. But you perceive the widening rift in the family lute. (*A silence* .) Pardon this glimpse into the secret history of the week.

HILDEGARDE (*formidably*). Mr. Tranto, you and I are sitting on the edge of a volcano.

TRANTO. We are. I like it. Thrilling, and yet so warm and cosy.

HILDEGARDE. I used to like it once. But I don't think I like it any more.

TRANTO. Now please don't let Auntie Joe worry you. She's my cross, not yours.

HILDEGARDE. Yes. But considered as a cross, your Auntie Joe is nothing to my brother John, who quite justly calls his sister's cookery stuff 'tripe.' It was a most ingenious camouflage of yours to have me pretending to be the author of that food economy 'tripe,' so as to cover my writing quite different articles for *The Echo* and your coming here to see me so often. Most ingenious. Worthy of a newspaper proprietor. But why should I be saddled with 'tripe' that isn't mine?

TRANTO. Why, indeed! Then you think we ought to encourage the volcano with a lighted match—and run?

HILDEGARDE. I'm ready if you are.

TRANTO. Oh! I'm ready. Secrecy was a great stunt at first. Letting out the secret will be an even greater stunt now. It'll make the finest newspaper story since the fearful fall of the last Cabinet. Sampson Straight—equals Miss Hildegarde Culver, the twenty-one year old daughter of the Controller of Accounts! Typist in the Food Department, by day! Journalistic genius by night! The terror of Ministers! Read by all London! Raised the circulation of *The Echo* two hundred per cent! Phenomenon unique in the annals of Fleet Street! (*In a different tone, noticing* Hildegarde's *face*). Crude headlines, I admit, but that's what Uncle Joe has brought us to. We have to compete with Uncle Joe....

HILDEGARDE. Of course I shall have to leave home.

TRANTO. Leave home!

HILDEGARDE. Yes, and live by myself in rooms.

TRANTO. But why?

HILDEGARDE. I couldn't possibly stay here. Think how it would compromise father with the War Cabinet if I did. It might ruin him. And as accounts are everything in modern warfare, it might lose the war. But that's nothing—it's mamma I'm thinking of. Do you forget that Sampson Straight, being a young woman of advanced ideas, has written about everything, *everything* —yes, and several other subjects besides? For instance, here's the article I was revising when you came in. (*Shows the title-page to* Tranto.)

TRANTO. Splendid! You're the most courageous creature I ever met.

HILDEGARDE. Possibly. But not courageous enough to offer to kiss mamma when I went to bed on the night that *that (indicating the article*) had appeared in print under my own name. You don't know mamma.

TRANTO. But dash it! You could eat your mother!

HILDEGARDE. Pardon me. The contrary is the fact. Mamma could eat me.

TRANTO. But you're the illustrious Sampson Straight. There's more intelligence in your little finger than there is in your mother's whole body. See how you write.

HILDEGARDE. Write! I only began to write as a relief from mamma. I escaped secretly into articles like escaping into an underground passage. But as for facing mamma in the open!… Even father scarcely ever does that; and when he does, we hold our breath, and the cook turns teetotal. It wouldn't be the slightest use me trying to explain the situation logically to mamma. She wouldn't understand. She's far too clever to understand anything she doesn't like. Perhaps that's the secret of her power. No, if the truth about Sampson Straight is to come out I must leave home—quietly but firmly leave home. And why not? I can keep myself in splendour on Sampson's earnings. And the break is bound to come sooner or later. I admit I didn't begin very seriously, but reading my own articles has gradually made me serious. I feel I have a cause. A cause may be inconvenient, but it's magnificent. It's like champagne or high heels, and one must be prepared to suffer for it.

TRANTO. Cause be hanged! Suffer be hanged! High heels be hanged! Champagne—(*stops*). Miss Culver, if a disclosure means your leaving home I won't agree to any disclosure whatever. I will—not—agree. We'll sit tight on the volcano.

HILDEGARDE. But why won't you agree?

TRANTO (*excited*). Why won't I agree! Why won't I agree! Because I don't want you to leave home. I know you're a born genius—a marvel, a miracle, a prodigy, an incredible orchid, the most brilliant journalist in London. I'm fully aware of all that. But I do not and will not see you as a literary bachelor living with a cause and holding receptions of serious people in chambers furnished by Roger Fry. I like to think of you at home, here, in this charming atmosphere, amid the delightful vicissitudes of family existence, and—well, I like to think of you as a woman.

HILDEGARDE (*calmly and teasingly*). Mr. Tranto, we are forgetting one thing.

TRANTO. What's that?

HILDEGARDE. You're an editor, and I'm a contributor whom you've never met.

Enter Mrs. Culver (*L*).

MRS. CULVER. Mr. Tranto, how are you? (*Shaking hands* .) I'm delighted to see you. So sorry I didn't warn you we dine half an hour later—thanks to the scandalous way the Government slave-drives my poor husband. Please do excuse me. (*She sits*).

TRANTO. On the contrary, it's I who should ask to be excused—proposing myself like this at the last moment.

MRS. CULVER. It was very nice of you to think of us. Come and sit down here. (*Indicating a place by her side on the sofa* .) Now in my poor addled brain I had an idea you were engaged for to-night at your aunt's, Lady Blackfriars'.

TRANTO (*sitting*). Mrs. Culver, you forget nothing. I *was* engaged for Auntie Joe's, but she's ill and she's put me off.

MRS. CULVER. Dear me! How very sudden!

TRANTO. Sudden?

MRS. CULVER. I met Lady Blackfriars at tea late this afternoon and it struck me how well she was looking.

TRANTO. Yes, she always looks particularly well just before she's going to be ill. She's very brave, very brave.

MRS. CULVER. D'you mean in having twins? It was more than brave of her; it was beautiful—both boys, too.

HILDEGARDE (*innocently*). Budgeting for a long war.

MRS. CULVER (*affectionately*). My dear girl! Come here, darling, you haven't changed. Excuse me, Mr. Tranto.

HILDEGARDE (*approaching*). I've been so busy. And I thought nobody was coming.

MRS. CULVER. Is your father nobody? (*stroking and patting* Hildegarde's *dress into order*). What have you been so busy on?

HILDEGARDE. Article for *The Echo* . (Tranto, *who has been holding the MS., indicates it* .)

MRS. CULVER. I do wish you would let me see those cookery articles of yours before they're printed.

TRANTO (*putting MS. in his pocket*). I'm afraid that's quite against the rules. You see, in Fleet Street—

MRS. CULVER (*very pleasantly*). As you please. I don't pretend to be intellectual. But I confess I'm just a wee bit disappointed in Hildegarde's cookery articles. I'm a great believer in good cookery. I put it next to the Christian religion—and far in front of mere cleanliness. I've just been trying to read Professor Metchnikoff's wonderful book on 'The Nature of Man.' It only confirms me in my lifelong belief that until the nature of man is completely altered good cooking is the chief thing that women ought to understand. Now I taught Hildegarde some cookery myself. She was not what I should call a brilliant pupil, but she did grasp the great eternal principles. And yet I find her writing (*with charm and benevolence*) stuff like her last article—'The Everlasting Boiled Potato,' I think she called it. Hildegarde, it was really very naughty of you to say what you said in that article. (*Drawing down* Hildegarde's *head and kissing her* .)

TRANTO. Now why, Mrs. Culver? I thought it was so clever.

MRS. CULVER. It may be clever to advocate fried potatoes and chip potatoes and sauté potatoes as a change from the everlasting boiled. I daresay it's what you call journalism. But how can you fry potatoes without fat?

TRANTO. Ah! How?

MRS. CULVER. And where are you to obtain fat? *I* can't obtain fat. I stand in queues for hours because my servants won't—it's the latest form of democracy—but *I* can't obtain fat. I think the nearest fat is at Stratford-on-Avon.

TRANTO. Stand in queues! Mrs. Culver, you make me feel very guilty, plunging in at a moment's notice and demanding a whole dinner in a fatless world. I shall eat nothing but dry bread.

MRS. CULVER. We never serve bread at lunch or dinner unless it's specially asked for. But if soup, macaroni, eggs, and jelly will keep you alive till breakfast—

HILDEGARDE. But there's beefsteak, mamma—I've told Mr. Tranto.

MRS. CULVER. Only a little, and that's for your father. Beefsteak's the one thing that keeps off his neuralgia, Mr. Tranto. (*With apologetic persuasiveness* .) I'm sure you'll understand.

TRANTO. Dear lady, I've never had neuralgia in my life. Macaroni, eggs, and jelly are my dream. I've always wanted to feel like an invalid.

MRS. CULVER. And how did you get on with your Medical Board this morning?

TRANTO. How marvellous of you to remember that I had a Medical Board this morning! I believe I've found out your secret, Mrs. Culver—you're undergoing a course of Pelman with those sixty generals and forty admirals.

14

Well, the Medical Board have given me a new complaint. You'll be sorry to hear that I'm deformed.

MRS. CULVER. Not deformed!

TRANTO. Yes. It appears I'm flat-footed. (*Extending his leg* .) Have I ever told you that I had a dashing military career extending over four months, three of which I spent in hospital for a disease I hadn't got? Then I was discharged as unfit. After a year they raked me in again. Since then I've been boarded five times, and on the unimpeachable authority of various R.A.M.C. Colonels I've been afflicted with valvular disease of the heart, incipient tuberculosis, rickets, varicose veins, diabetes—practically everything, except spotted fever and leprosy. And now flat feet are added to all the rest. Even the Russian collapse and the transfer of the entire German army to the Western Front hasn't raised me higher than C 3.

MRS. CULVER. How annoying for you! You might have risen to be a captain by this time.

HILDEGARDE (*reflectively*). No doubt, in a home unit. But if he'd gone to the Front he would still have been a second lieutenant.

MRS. CULVER. My *dear* !

TRANTO. Whereas in fact I'm still one of those able-bodied young shirkers in mufti that patriotic old gentlemen in clubs are always writing to my uncles' papers about.

MRS. CULVER. Please! please! (*A slight pause; pulling herself together; cheerfully* .) Let me see, you were going in for Siege Artillery, weren't you?

TRANTO. Me! Siege Artillery. My original ambition was trench mortars—not so noisy.

MRS. CULVER (*simply*). Oh! Then it must have been somebody else who was talking to me about Siege Artillery. I understand it's very scientific—all angles and degrees and wind-pressures and things. John will soon be eighteen, and his father and I want him to be really useful in the Army. We don't want him to be thrown away. He has brains, and so we are thinking of Siege Artillery for him.

(*During this speech* John *has entered, in evening dress* .)

JOHN. Are you on Siege again, mater? The mater's keen on Siege because she's heard somewhere it's the safest thing there is.

MRS. CULVER. And if it does happen to be the safest—what then?

TRANTO. I suppose you're all for the Flying Corps, John?

JOHN (*with condescension*). Not specially. Since one of the old boys came and did looping the loop stunts over the school the whole Fifth has gone mad on the R.F.C. Most fellows are just like sheep. *Somebody* in the Sixth has to be original. I want to fight as much as any chap with wings across his chest, but I've got my private career to think of too. If you ask me, the mater's had a brain-wave for once.

Enter Mr. Culver, *back. He stands a moment at the door, surveying the scene .* Mrs. Culver *springs up, and* Tranto *also rises, moving towards the door .*

MRS. CULVER. Arthur, have you come?

CULVER (*advancing a little*). Apparently. Hello, Tranto, glad to see you. I wanted to. (*Shakes hands with* Tranto.)

MRS. CULVER. What's the matter, Arthur?

CULVER. Everything.

MRS. CULVER (*alarmed, but carefully coaxing*). Why are you wearing your velvet coat? (*To* Tranto.) He always puts on his velvet coat instead of dressing when something's gone wrong. (*To* Mr. Culver.) Have you got neuralgia again?

CULVER. I don't think so.

MRS. CULVER. But surely you must know! You look terribly pale.

CULVER. The effect of the velvet coat, my dear—nicely calculated in advance.

MRS. CULVER (*darting at him, holding him by the shoulders, and then kissing him violently. With an intonation of affectionate protest*). Darling!

JOHN. Oh! I say, mater, look here!

MRS. CULVER (*to* Culver, *still holding him*). I'm very annoyed with you. It's perfectly absurd the way you work. (*To* Tranto.) Do you know he was at the office all day Christmas Day and all day Boxing Day? (*To* Culver.) You really must take a holiday.

CULVER. But what about the war, darling?

MRS. CULVER (*loosing him*). Oh! You're always making the war an excuse. I know what I shall do. I shall just go—

CULVER. Yes, darling, just go and suggest a short armistice to the Germans while you take me to Brighton for a week's fondling.

MRS. CULVER. I shall just speak to Miss Starkey. Strange that the wife, in order to influence the husband, should have to appeal to (*disdainfully*) the lady secretary! But so it is.

CULVER. Hermione, I must beg you not to interfere between Miss Starkey and me. Interference will upset Miss Starkey, and I cannot stand her being upset. I depend upon her absolutely. First, Miss Starkey is the rock upon which my official existence is built. She is a serious and conscientious rock. She is hard and expects me to be hard. Secondly, Miss Starkey is the cushion between me and the world. She knows my tender spots, and protects them. Thirdly, Miss Starkey is my rod—and I kiss it.

MRS. CULVER. Arthur!… (*tries to be agreeable*). But I really am vexed.

CULVER. Well, I'm only hungry.

Enter Parlourmaid.

PARLOURMAID. Cook's compliments, madam, and dinner will be twenty minutes late. (*Exit* .)

(*A shocked silence* .)

CULVER (*with an exhausted sigh*). And yet I gave that cook one of my most captivating smiles this morning.

MRS. CULVER (*settling* Mr. Culver *into a chair*). She's done it simply because I told her to-night that rationing is definitely coming in. Her reply was that the kitchen would never stand it, whatever the Government said. She was quite upset—and so she's gone and done something to the dinner.

CULVER. Surely rather illogical of her, isn't it? Or have I missed a link in the chain of reasoning?

MRS. CULVER. I shall give her notice—after dinner.

JOHN. Couldn't you leave it till after the holidays, mother?

HILDEGARDE. And where shall you find another cook, mamma?

MRS. CULVER. The first thing is to get rid of the present one. Then we shall see.

CULVER. My dear, you talk as if she was a prime minister. Still, it might be a good plan to sack all the servants before rationing comes in, and engage deaf-mutes.

MRS. CULVER. Deaf-mutes!

CULVER. Deaf-mutes. Then they wouldn't be worried by the continual groaning of *my* hunger, and I shouldn't hear any complaints about *theirs* .

MRS. CULVER (*to* Hildegarde). My pet, you've time to change now. Do run and change. You're so sombre.

HILDEGARDE. I can't do it in twenty minutes.

MRS. CULVER. Then put a bright shawl on—for papa's sake.

HILDEGARDE. I haven't got a bright shawl.

MRS. CULVER. Then take mine. The one with the pink beads on it. It's in my wardrobe—right-hand side.

JOHN. That means it'll be on the left-hand side.

(*Exit* Hildegarde, *back, with a look at Tranto, who opens the door for her* .)

MRS. CULVER (*with sweet apprehensiveness*). Now Arthur, I'm afraid after all you have something on your mind.

CULVER. I've got nothing on my stomach, anyway. (*Bracing himself* .) Yes, darling, it's true. I have got something on my mind. Within the last hour I've had a fearful shock—

MRS. CULVER. I knew it!

CULVER. And I need sustaining. I hadn't meant to say anything until after dinner, but in view of cook's drastic alterations in the time-table I may as well tell you (*looking round*) at once.

MRS. CULVER. It's something about the Government again.

CULVER. The Government has been in a very serious situation.

MRS. CULVER (*alarmed*). You mean they're going to ask you to resign?

CULVER. I wish they would!

MRS. CULVER. Arthur! Do please remember the country is at war.

CULVER. Is it? So it is. You see, my pet, I remember such a lot of things. I remember that my brainy partner is counting khaki trousers in the Army clothing department. I remember that my other partner ought to be in a lunatic asylum, but isn't. I remember that my business is going to the dogs at a muzzle velocity of about five thousand feet a second. I remember that from mere snobbishness I work for the Government without a penny of salary, and that my sole reward is to be insulted and libelled by high-brow novelists who write for the press. Therefore you ought not to be startled if I secretly yearn to resign. However, I shall not be asked to resign. I said that the Government had been in a very serious situation. It was. But it will soon recover.

MRS. CULVER. How soon?

CULVER. On New Year's Day.

JOHN. Then what's the fearful shock, dad?

MRS. CULVER. Yes. Have you heard anything special?

CULVER. No. But I've seen something special. I saw it less than an hour ago. It was shown to me without the slightest warning, and I admit it shook me. You can perceive for yourselves that it shook me.

MRS. CULVER. But what?

CULVER. The New Year's Honours List—or rather a few choice selections from the more sensational parts of it.

Enter Hildegarde.

MRS. CULVER. Arthur, *what* do you mean? (*To* Hildegarde, *in despair* .) My chick, your father grows more and more puzzling every day! How well that shawl suits you! You look quite a different girl. But you've—(*arranges the shawl on* Hildegarde) I really don't know what your father has on his mind! I really don't!

JOHN (*impatient of this feminine manifestation*). Oh, dad, go on. Go on! I want to get at the bottom of this titles business. I'm hanged if I can understand it. What strikes me as an unprejudiced observer is that titles are supposed to be such a terrific honour, and yet the people who deal them out scarcely ever keep any for themselves. Look at Mr. Gladstone, for instance. He must have made about forty earls and seven thousand baronets in his time. Now if I was a Prime Minister, and I believed in titles—which I jolly well don't—I should make myself a duke right off; and I should have several marquises and viscounts round me in the Cabinet like a sort of bodyguard, and my private secretaries would have to be knights. There'd be some logic in that arrangement anyhow.

CULVER. In view of your political career, John, will you mind if I give you a brief lesson on elementary politics—though you *are* on your holidays?

JOHN (*easily*). I'm game.

CULVER. What is the first duty of modern Governments?

JOHN. To govern.

CULVER. My innocent boy. I thought better of you. I know that you look on the venerable Mr. Tranto as a back number, and I suspect that Mr. Tranto in his turn regards me as prehistoric; and yet you are so behind the times as to imagine that the first duty of modern Governments is to govern! My dear Rip van Winkle, wake up. The first duty of a Government is to live. It has no right to be a Government at all unless it is convinced that if it fell the country would go to everlasting smash. Hence its first duty is to survive. In order to survive it must do three things—placate certain interests, influence votes, and obtain secret funds. All these three things can be accomplished by the ingenious institution of Honours. Only the simple-minded believe that Honours are given to honour. Honours are given to save the life of the Government. Hence the Honours List. Examine the Honours List and you can instantly tell how the Government feels in its inside. When the Honours List is full of rascals, millionaires, and—er—chumps, you may be quite sure that the Government is dangerously ill.

TRANTO. But that amounts to what we've been saying in *The Echo* to-day.

CULVER. Yes, I've read the *The Echo* .

JOHN. I thought you never had a free moment at the office—always rushed to death—at least that's the mater's theory.

CULVER. I've read *The Echo* , and my one surprise is that you're here to-night, Tranto.

TRANTO. Why?

CULVER. I quite thought you'd have been shoved into the Tower under the Defence of the Realm Act. Or Sampson Straight, anyway. (Hildegarde *starts* .) Your contributor has committed the unpardonable sin of hitting the nail on the head. He might almost have seen an advance copy of the Honours List.

TRANTO. He hadn't. Nor had I. Who's in it?

CULVER. You might ask who isn't in it. (*Taking a paper from his pocket* .) Well, Gentletie's in it. He gets a knighthood.

TRANTO. Never heard of him. Who is he?

HILDEGARDE. Oh, yes, you've heard of him. (John *glances at her severely* .) He's M.P. for some earthly paradise or other in the South Riding.

TRANTO. Oh!

CULVER. Perhaps I might read you something written by my private secretary—he's one of these literary wags. You see there's been a demand that the Government should state clearly, in every case of an Honour, exactly what services the Honour is given for. This (*taking paper from his pocket*) is supposed to be the stuff sent round to the Press by the Press Bureau. (*Reads* .) 'Mr. Gentletie has gradually made a solid reputation for himself as the dullest man in the House of Commons. Whenever he rises to his feet the House empties as if by magic. In cases of inconvenience, when the Government wishes abruptly to close a debate by counting out the House, it has invariably put up Mr. Gentletie to speak. The device has never been known to fail. Nobody can doubt that Mr. Gentletie's patriotic devotion to the

Allied cause well merits the knighthood which is now bestowed on him.'

JOHN (*astounded* .) Stay me with flagons!

TRANTO. So that's that! And who else?

CULVER. Another of your esteemed uncles.

TRANTO. Well, that's not very startling, seeing that my uncle's chief daily organ is really a department of the Government.

JOHN. What I say is—

HILDEGARDE (*simultaneously with* John). Wouldn't it be more correct—(*continuing alone*) wouldn't it be more correct to say that the Government is really a department of your uncle's chief daily organ?

JOHN. Hilda, old girl, I wish you wouldn't interrupt. Cookery's your line.

HILDEGARDE. Sorry, Johnnie. I see I was in danger of becoming unsexed.

CULVER (*to* John). Yes? You were about to say?

JOHN. Oh, nothing.

CULVER (*to* Tranto). Shall I read the passage on your uncle?

TRANTO. Don't trouble. Who's the next?

CULVER. The next is—Ullivant, munitions manufacturer. Let me see. (*Reads* .) By the simple means of saying that the cost price of shells was eighteen shillings and ninepence each, whereas it was in fact only ten shillings and ninepence, Mr. Joshua Ullivant has made a fortune of two million pounds during the war. He has given a hundred thousand to the Prince of Wales's Fund, a hundred thousand to the Red Cross, and a hundred thousand to the party funds. Total net profit on the war, one million seven hundred thousand pounds, not counting the peerage which is now bestowed upon him, and which it must be admitted is a just reward for his remarkable business acumen.'

TRANTO. Very agreeable fellow Ullivant is, nevertheless.

CULVER. Oh, he is. They're most of them too damned agreeable for anything. Another prominent name is Orlando Bush.

TRANTO. Ah!

MRS. CULVER. I've met his wife. She dances beautifully at charity matinees.

CULVER. No doubt. But apparently that's not the reason.

TRANTO. I know Orlando. I've just bought the serial rights of his book.

CULVER. Have you paid him?

TRANTO. No.

CULVER. How wise of you! (*Reads*). 'Mr. Orlando Bush has written a historical sketch, with many circumstantial details, of the political origins of the present Government. For his forbearance in kindly consenting to withold publication until the end of the war Mr. Bush receives a well-earned'—

TRANTO. What?

CULVER. Knighthood.

TRANTO. Cheap! But what a sell for me!

CULVER. Now, ladies and gentlemen, the last name with which I will trouble you is that of Mr. James Brill.

TRANTO. Not Jimmy Brill!

CULVER. Jimmy Brill.

TRANTO. But he's a—

CULVER. Stop, my dear Tranto. No crude phrases, please. (*Reads* .) 'Mr. James Brill, to use the language of metaphor, possessed a pistol, which pistol he held point blank at the head of the Government. The Government has thought it wise to purchase Mr. James Brill's pistol—'

TRANTO. But he's a—

CULVER (*raising a hand*). He is merely the man with the pistol, and in exchange for the pistol he gets a baronetcy.

TRANTO. A baronetcy!

CULVER. His title and pistol will go rattling down the ages, my dear Tranto, from generation to generation. For the moment the fellow's name stinks, but only for the moment. In the nostrils of his grandson (third baronet), it will have a most sweet odour.

MRS. CULVER. But all this is perfectly shocking.

CULVER. Now I hope you comprehend my emotion, darling.

MRS. CULVER But surely there are some *nice* names on the List.

CULVER. Of course. There have to be some nice names, for the sake of the psychological effect on the public mind on New Year's Day. The public looks for a good name, or for a name it can understand. It skims down the List till it sees one. Then it says: 'Ah! That's not so bad!' Then it skims down further till it sees another one, and it says again: 'Ah! That's not so bad!' And so on. So that with about five or six decent names you can produce the illusion that after all the List is really rather good.

HILDEGARDE. The strange thing to me is that decent people condescend to receive titles at all.

MRS. CULVER. Bravo, Hildegarde! Yes, if it's so bad as you make out, Arthur, why *do* decent people take Honours?

CULVER. I'll tell you. Decent people have wives, and their wives lead them by the nose. That's why decent people take Honours.

MRS. CULVER. Well, I think it's monstrous!

CULVER. So it is. I've been a Conservative all my life; I am a Conservative. I swear I am. And yet, now when I look back, I'm amazed at the things I used to do. Why, once I actually voted against a candidate who stood for the reform of the House of Lords. Seems incredible. This war is changing my ideas. (*Suddenly, after a slight pause* .) I'm dashed if I don't join the Labour party and ask Ramsay Macdonald to lunch.

Enter Parlourmaid, *back* .

PARLOURMAID. You are wanted on the telephone, madam.

MRS. CULVER. Oh, Arthur! (*Pats him on the shoulder as she goes out* .)

(*Exit* Mrs. Culver *and* Parlourmaid, *back* .)

CULVER. Hildegarde, go and see if you can hurry up dinner.

HILDEGARDE. No one could.

CULVER. Never mind, go and see. (*Exit* Hildegarde, *back* .) John, just take these keys, and get some cigars out of the cabinet, you know, Partagas.

JOHN. Oh! Is it a Partaga night? (*Exit, back* .)

CULVER (*watching the door close*). Tranto, we are conspirators.

TRANTO. You and I?

CULVER. Yes. But we must have no secrets. Who wrote that article in *The Echo* ? Who is Sampson Straight?

TRANTO (*temporising, lightly*). You remind me of the man with the pistol.

CULVER. Is it Hildegarde?

TRANTO. How did you guess?

23

CULVER. Well; first, I knew my daughter couldn't be the piffling lunatic who does your war cookery articles. Second, I asked myself: What reason has she for pretending to be that piffling lunatic? Third, I have an exceedingly high opinion of my daughter's brains. Fourth, she gave a funny start just now when I mentioned the idea of Sampson Straight going to the Tower.

TRANTO. Perhaps I ought to explain—

CULVER. No you oughn't. There's no time. I simply wanted a bit of information. I've got it. Now I have a bit of information for you. I've been offered a place in this beautiful Honours List. Baronetcy! Me! I am put on the same high plane as Mr. James Brill, the unspeakable. The formal offer hasn't actually arrived—it's late; I expect the letter'll be here in the morning—but I know for a fact I'm in the List for a baronetcy.

TRANTO. Well, I congratulate you.

CULVER. You'd better not.

TRANTO. You deserve more than a baronetcy. Your department has been a striking success—one of the very few in the whole length of Whitehall.

CULVER. I know my department has been a success. But that's not why I'm offered a baronetcy. Good heavens, I haven't even spoken to any member of the War Cabinet yet. I've been trying to for about a year, but in spite of powerful influences to help me I've never been able to bring off a meeting with the mandarins. No! I'm offered a baronetcy because I'm respectable; I'm decent; and at the last moment they thought the List looked a bit too thick— so they pushed me in. One of their brilliant afterthoughts!… No damned merit about the thing, I can tell you!

TRANTO. Do you mean you intend to refuse?

CULVER. Do you mean you ever imagined that I should accept? Me, in the same galley with Brill—who daren't go into his own clubs—and Ullivant, and a few more pretty nearly as bad! Of course, I shall refuse. Nothing on earth would induce me to accept. Nothing! (*More calmly* .) Mind you, I don't blame the Government; probably the Government can't help itself. Therefore the Government must be helped; and sometimes the best way to help a fellow creature is to bring him to his senses by catching him one across the jaw.

TRANTO. Why are you making a secret of it? The offer is surely bound to come out.

CULVER. Of course. I'm only making a secret of it for the moment, while I prepare the domestic ground for my refusal.

TRANTO. You wish me to understand—

CULVER. You know what women are. (*With caution* .) I speak of the sex in general.

TRANTO. I see.

CULVER. That's all right.

TRANTO. Well, if I mayn't congratulate you on the title, let me congratulate you on your marvellous skill in this delicate operation of preparing the domestic ground for your refusal of the title. Your success is complete, absolute.

CULVER (*sardonic* .) Complete? Absolute?

TRANTO. You have—er—jockeyed Mrs.—er—the sex into committing itself quite definitely against titles. Hence I look on your position as impregnable.

CULVER. Good heavens, Tranto! How old are you?

TRANTO. Twenty-five.

CULVER. A quarter of a century—and you haven't learnt that no position is impregnable against—er—the sex! You never know where the offensive will come, nor when, nor how. The offensive is bound to be a surprise. You aren't married. When you are you'll soon find out that being a husband is a whole-time job. That's why so many husbands fail. They can't give their entire attention to it. Tranto, my position must be still further strengthened—during dinner. It can't be strengthened too much. I've brought you into the conspiracy because you're on the spot and I want you to play up.

TRANTO. Certainly, sir.

CULVER. The official letter *might* come by to-night's post. If it does, a considerable amount of histrionic skill will be needed.

TRANTO. Trust me for that.

CULVER. Oh! I do! Indeed I fancy after all I'm fairly safe. There's only one danger.

TRANTO. Yes?

CULVER. My—I mean the sex, must hear of the offered title from me first. If the news came to her indirectly she'd—

Enter Mrs. Culver *rapidly, back* .

MRS. CULVER (*rushing to him*). Darling! Dearest! What a tease you are! You needn't pretend any longer. Lady Prockter has just whispered to me over the telephone that you're to have a baronetcy. Of course she'd be bound to know. She said I might tell you. I never *dreamed* of a title. I'm so glad. Oh!

25

But you *are* a tease! (*Kisses him enthusiastically* .)

CURTAIN.

ACT II

ACT II

The next day after dinner . Culver *and* Parlourmaid.

CULVER (*handing* Parlourmaid *a letter*). That's for the post. Is Miss Starkey here?

PARLOURMAID. Yes, sir. She is waiting.

CULVER. Ask her to be good enough to keep on waiting. She may come in when I ring twice.

PARLOURMAID. Yes, sir.

Enter Mrs. Culver, *back* .

MRS. CULVER (*to* Parlourmaid, *stopping her as she goes out, dramatically*). Give me that letter. (*She snatches the letter from the* Parlourmaid.) You can go. (Culver *rises* .) (*Exit* Parlourmaid.)

MRS. CULVER. I am determined to make a stand this time.

CULVER (*soothingly*). So I see, darling.

MRS. CULVER. I have given way to you all my life. But I won't give way now. This letter shall not go.

CULVER. As you like, darling.

MRS. CULVER. No. (*She tears the envelope open, without having looked at it, and throws the letter into the fire. In doing so she lets fall a cheque* .)

CULVER (*rising and picking up the cheque*). I'll keep the cheque as a memento.

MRS. CULVER. Cheque? What cheque?

CULVER. Darling, once in the old, happy days—I think it was last week— you and I were walking down Bond Street, almost hand in hand, but not quite, and you saw a brooch in a shop window. You simply had to have that brooch. I offered it to you for a Christmas present. You are wearing it now, and very well it suits you. This (*indicating the cheque*) was to pay the bill.

MRS. CULVER. Arthur!

CULVER. Moral: Look before you burn. Miss Starkey will now have to write a fresh letter.

MRS. CULVER. Arthur! You must forgive me. I'm in a horrid state of nerves, and you said you were positively going to write to Lord Woking to-night to refuse the title.

CULVER. I did say so.

MRS. CULVER (*hopefully*). But you haven't written?

CULVER. I haven't.

MRS. CULVER. You don't know how relieved I am!

CULVER (*sitting down, drawing her to him, and setting her on his knee*). Infant! Cherub! Angel! Dove!... Devil! (*Caressing her* .) Are we friends?

MRS. CULVER. It kills me to quarrel with you. (*They kiss* .)

CULVER. Darling, we are absurd.

MRS. CULVER. I don't care.

CULVER. Supposing that anyone came in and caught us!

MRS. CULVER. Well, we're married.

CULVER.—But it's so long since. Hildegarde's twenty-one! John, seventeen!

MRS. CULVER. It seems to me like yesterday.

CULVER. Yes, you're incurably a girl.

MRS. CULVER. I'm not.

CULVER. You are. And I'm a boy. I say we are absurd. We're continually absurd. We were absurd all last evening when we pretended before the others, with the most disastrous results, that nothing was the matter. We were still more absurd when we went to our twin beds and argued savagely with each other from bed to bed until four o'clock this morning. Do you know that I had exactly one hour and fifty-five minutes' sleep? (*Yawns* .) Do you know that owing to extreme exhaustion my behaviour at my office to-day has practically lost the war? But the most absurd thing of all was you trying to do the Roman matron business at dinner to-night. Mind you, I adore you for being absurd, but—

MRS. CULVER (*very endearingly, putting her hand on his mouth*). Dearest, you needn't continue. I know you're wiser and stronger than me in every way. But I love that. Most women wouldn't; but I do. (*Kisses him* .) Oh! I'm so glad you've at last seen the force of my arguments about the title.

CULVER (*gently warning*). Now, now! You're behaving like a journalist.

MRS. CULVER. Like a journalist?

CULVER. Journalists say a thing that they know isn't true, in the hope that if they keep on saying it long enough it *will* be true.

MRS. CULVER. But you do see the force of my arguments!

CULVER. Quite. But I also see the force of mine, and, as an impartial judge, I'm bound to say that yours aren't in it with mine.

MRS. CULVER. Then you've refused the title after all?

CULVER (*ingratiatingly*). No. I told you I hadn't. But I'm going to. I was just thinking over the terms of the fatal letter to Lord Woking when you came in. Starkey is now waiting for me to dictate it. You see it positively must be posted to-night.

MRS. CULVER (*springing from his knee*). Arthur, you're playing with me!

CULVER. No doubt. Like a mouse plays with a cat.

MRS. CULVER. Surely it has occurred to you—

CULVER (*firmly, but very pleasantly*). Stop! You had till four o'clock this morning to deliver all your arguments. You aren't going to begin again. I understand you've stayed in bed all day. Quite right! But if you stayed in bed merely to think of fresh arguments while I've been slaving away at the office for my country, I say you're taking an unfair advantage of me, and I won't have it.

MRS. CULVER (*with dignity*). No. I haven't any fresh arguments; and if I had, I shouldn't say what they were.

CULVER. Oh! Why?

MRS. CULVER. Because I can see it's useless to argue with a man like you.

CULVER. Now that's what I call better news from the Front.

MRS. CULVER. I was only going to say this. Surely it has occurred to you that on patriotic grounds alone you oughtn't to refuse the title. I quite agree that Honours have been degraded. Quite! The thing surely is to try and make them respectable again. And how are they ever to be respectable if respectable men refuse them?

CULVER. This looks to me suspiciously like an argument.

MRS. CULVER. Not at all. It's simply a question.

CULVER. Well, the answer is, I don't want Honours to be respectable any more. Proverb: When fish has gone bad ten thousand decent men can't take away the stink.

MRS. CULVER. Now you're insulting your country. I know you often pretend your country's the slackest place on earth, but it's only pretence. You don't really think so. The truth is that inside you you're positively conceited about your country. You think it's the greatest country that ever was. And so it is. And yet when your country offers you this honour you talk about bad fish. I say it's an insult to Great Britain.

CULVER. Great Britain hasn't offered me any title. The fact is that there are a couple of shrewd fellows up a devil of a tree in Whitehall, and they're waving a title at me in the hope that I shall come and stand under the tree so that they can get down by putting their dirty boots on my shoulders. Well, I'm not going to be a ladder.

MRS. CULVER. I wish you wouldn't try to be funny.

CULVER. I'm not *trying* to be funny. I *am* being funny.

MRS. CULVER. You might be serious for once.

CULVER. I am serious. Beneath this amusing and delightful exterior, there is hidden the most serious, determined, resolute, relentless, inexorable, immovable man that ever breathed. And let me tell you something else, my girl—something I haven't mentioned before because of my nice feelings. What has this title affair got to do with you? What the dickens has it got to do with you? The title isn't offered as a reward for *your* work; it's offered as a reward for *my* work. *You* aren't the Controller of Accounts, *I* happen to be the Controller of Accounts. I have decided to refuse the title, and I shall refuse it. *Nothing will induce me to accept it* . Do I make myself clear, or (*smiling affectionately*) am I lost in a mist of words?

MRS. CULVER (*suddenly furious*). You are a brute. You always were. You never think of anybody but yourself. My life has been one long sacrifice, and you know it perfectly well. Perfectly well! You talk about *your* work. What about my work? Why! You'd be utterly useless without me. You can't even look after your own collars. Could you go down to your ridiculous office without a collar? I've done everything for you, everything! And now! (*Weeping*). I can't even be called 'my lady.' I only wanted to hear the parlourmaid call me 'my lady.' It seems a simple enough thing—

CULVER (*persuasively and softly, trying to seize her*). You divine little snob!

MRS. CULVER (*in a supreme, blazing outbreak escaping him*). Let me alone! I told you at the start I should never give way. And I never will. Never! If you send that letter of refusal, do you know what I shall do? I shall go and see the War Cabinet myself. I shall tell them you don't mean it. I'll make the most horrible scandal…. When I think of the Duke of Wellington—

CULVER (*surprised and alarmed*). The Duke of Wellington?

MRS. CULVER (*drawing herself up at the door, L*). The Duke of Wellington didn't refuse a title! Hildegarde shall sleep in our room, and you can have hers! (*Exit violently, L* .)

CULVER (*intimidated, as she goes*). Look here, hurricane! (*He rushes out after her* .)

Enter Hildegarde *and* Tranto, *back* .

HILDEGARDE (*seeing the room empty*). Well, I thought I heard them.

TRANTO (*catching noise of high words from the boudoir* .) I fancy I *do* hear them.

HILDEGARDE. Perhaps we'd better go.

TRANTO. But I want to speak to you—just for a moment.

HILDEGARDE (*moving uneasily*). What about?

TRANTO. I don't know. Anything. It doesn't matter what … I don't hear them now.

HILDEGARDE (*listening and hearing nothing; reassured*). I should have thought you wouldn't have wanted to come here any more for a long time.

TRANTO. Why?

HILDEGARDE. After the terrible experiences of last night, during dinner and after dinner.

TRANTO. The general constraint?

HILDEGARDE. The general constraint.

TRANTO. The awkwardness? HILDEGARDE. The awkwardness.

TRANTO. The frightful silences and the forced conversations?

HILDEGARDE (*nods*). Why *did* you come?

TRANTO. Well—

HILDEGARDE. I suppose you're still confined to this house.

TRANTO (*in a new confidential tone*). I wish you'd treat me as your father does.

HILDEGARDE. But of course I will—

TRANTO. That's fine. He treats me as an intimate friend.

HILDEGARDE. But you must treat me as you treat papa.

TRANTO (*slightly dashed*). I'll try. I might tell you that I had two very straight talks with your father last night.

HILDEGARDE. Two?

TRANTO. Yes; one before dinner, and the other just before I left—when you'd gone to bed. He began them—both of them.

HILDEGARDE. Oh! So that you may be said to know the whole situation.

TRANTO. Yes. Up to last thing last night, that is.

HILDEGARDE. Since then it's developed on normal lines. What do you think of it?

TRANTO. I adore your mother, but I think your father's quite right.

HILDEGARDE. Well, naturally! I take that for granted. I was expecting something rather more original.

TRANTO. You shall have it. I think that you and I are very largely responsible for the situation. I think our joint responsibility binds us inextricably together.

HILDEGARDE. Mr. Tranto!

TRANTO. Certainly. There's no doubt in my mind that your father was enormously influenced by Sampson Straight's article on the Honours scandal. In fact he told me so. And seeing that you wrote it and I published it—

HILDEGARDE (*alarmed*). You didn't tell him I'm Sampson Straight?

TRANTO. Can you imagine me doing such a thing?

HILDEGARDE. I hope not. Shall I tell you what *I* think of the situation?

TRANTO. I wish you would.

HILDEGARDE. I think such situations would never arise if parents weren't so painfully unromantic. I'm not speaking particularly of papa and mamma. I mean all parents. But take mamma. She's absolutely matter-of-fact. And papa's nearly as bad. Of course I know they're always calling each other by pet names; but that's mere camouflage for their matter-of-factness. Whereas if they both had in them a little of the real romance of life—everything would be different. At the same time I needn't say that in this affair that we're now in the middle of—there's no question of ratiocination.

TRANTO. Of what?

HILDEGARDE. Ratiocination. Reasoning. On either side.

TRANTO. Oh no!

HILDEGARDE. It's simply a question of mutual attitude, isn't it? Now, if only—. But there! What's the use? Parents are like that, poor dears! They have forgotten! (*With emphasis* .) They have forgotten—what makes life worth living.

TRANTO. You mean, for instance, your mother never sits on your father's knee.

HILDEGARDE (*bravely, after hesitation*). Yes! Crudely—that's what I do mean.

TRANTO. Miss Hildegarde, you are the most marvellous girl I ever met. You are, really! You seem to combine all qualities. It's amazing to me. I'm more and more astounded. Every time I come here there's a fresh revelation. Now you mention romance. I'm glad you mentioned it first. But I *saw* it first. I saw it in your eyes the first time I ever met you. Yes! Miss Hilda, do you see it in mine? Look. Look closely. (*Approaching her* .) Because it's there. I must tell you. I can't wait any longer. (*Feeling for her hand, vainly* .)

HILDEGARDE (*drawing back*). Mr. Tranto, is this the way you treat father?

Enter Mr. Culver, *back* .

CULVER (*quickly*). Hilda, go to your mother. She's upstairs.
HILDEGARDE. What am I to do?

CULVER. I don't know. (*With meaning* .) Think what the sagacious Sampson Straight would do, and do that.

(Hildegarde *gives a sharp look first at* Culver, *and then at* Tranto, *and exit, back* .)

CULVER (*turning to* Tranto). My dear fellow, the war is practically over.

TRANTO. Good heavens! There was nothing on the tape when I left the Club.

CULVER. Oh! I don't mean your war. I mean the twenty-two years' war.

TRANTO. The twenty-two years' war?

CULVER. My married life. Over! Finished! Napoo!

TRANTO. Do you know what you're saying?

CULVER. Look here, Tranto. You and I don't belong to the same generation. In fact, if I'd started early enough I might have been your father. But we got so damned intimate last night, and I'm in such a damned hole, and you're so damned wise, that I feel I must talk to you. Not that it'll be any use.

TRANTO. But what's the matter?

CULVER. The matter is—keeping a woman in the house.

TRANTO. Mr. Culver! You don't mean—

CULVER. I mean my wife—of course. I've just had the most ghastly rumpus with my wife. It was divided into two acts. The first took place here, the second in the boudoir (*indicating boudoir*). The second act was the shortest but the worst.

TRANTO. But what was it all about?

CULVER. Now for heaven's sake don't ask silly questions. You know perfectly well what it was about. It was about the baronetcy. I have decided to refuse that baronetcy, and my wife has refused to let me refuse it.

TRANTO. But what are her arguments?

CULVER. I've implored you once not to ask silly questions. 'What are her arguments' indeed! She hasn't got any arguments. You know that. You're too wise not to know it. She merely wants the title, that's all.

TRANTO. And how did the second act end?

CULVER. I don't quite remember.

TRANTO. Let me suggest that you sit down. (Culver *sits* .) Thanks. Now I've always gathered from my personal observation, that you, if I may say so, are the top dog here when it comes to the point—the crowned head, as it were.

35

CULVER. Uneasy lies the head that wears a crown. At least, it did last night, and I shall be greatly surprised if it doesn't to-night.

TRANTO. Naturally. A crown isn't a night-cap. But you are the top dog. In the last resort, what you say, goes. That is so, isn't it? I only want to be clear.

CULVER. Yes, I think that's pretty right.

TRANTO. Well, you have decided on public grounds, and as a question of principle, to refuse the title. You intend to refuse it.

CULVER. I—I do.

TRANTO. Nobody can stop you from refusing it.

CULVER. Nobody.

TRANTO. Mrs. Culver can't stop you from refusing it?

CULVER. Certainly not. It concerns me alone.

TRANTO. Well, then, where is the difficulty? A rumpus—I think you said. What of that? My dear Mr. Culver, believe me, I have seen far more of marriage than you have. You're only a married man. I'm a bachelor, and I've assisted at scores of married lives. A rumpus is nothing. It passes—and leaves the victor more firmly established than ever before.

CULVER (*rising*). Don't talk to me of rumpuses. I know all about rumpuses. This one is an arch-rumpus. This one is like no other rumpus that ever was. It's something new in my vast experience. I shall win. I have won. But at what cost? (*With effect* .) The cost may be that I shall never kiss the enemy again. The whole domestic future is in grave jeopardy.

TRANTO. Seriously?

CULVER. Seriously.

TRANTO. Then you musn't win.

CULVER. But what about my public duty? What about my principles? I can't sacrifice my principles.

TRANTO. Why not?

CULVER. I never have.

TRANTO. How old are you?

CULVER. Forty-four.

TRANTO. And you've never sacrificed a principle?

CULVER. Never.

TRANTO. Then it's high time you began. And you'd better begin, before it's too late. Besides, there are no principles in married life.

CULVER. Tranto, you are remarkable. How did you find that out?

TRANTO. I've often noticed it.

CULVER. It's a profound truth. It throws a new light on the entire situation.

TRANTO. It does.

CULVER. Then you deliberately advise me to give way about the title?

TRANTO. I do.

CULVER. Strange! (*Casually* .) I had thought of doing so, but I never dreamt you'd agree, and I'd positively determined to act on your advice. You know, you're taking an immense responsibility.

TRANTO. I can bear that. What I couldn't bear is any kind of real trouble in this house.

CULVER. Why? What's it got to do with you?

TRANTO. Nothing! Nothing! Only my abstract interest in the institution of marriage.

CULVER (*ringing the bell twice*). Ah, well, after all, I'm not utterly beaten yet. I've quite half an hour before post goes, and I shall fight to the last ditch.

TRANTO. But hasn't Mrs. Culver retired?

CULVER. Yes.

TRANTO. May I suggest that it would be mistaken tactics to—er—run after her?

CULVER. It would.

TRANTO. Well then?

CULVER. She will return.

TRANTO. How do you know?

CULVER. She always does…. No, Tranto, I may yet get peace on my own terms. You see I'm an accountant. No ordinary people, accountants! For one thing they make their money by counting other people's. I've known accountants do marvellous stunts.

Enter Miss Starkey, *back* .

TRANTO. I'll leave you.

37

CULVER. You'll find John somewhere about. I shan't be so very long—I hope. Miss Starkey, kindly take down these two letters. How much time have we before post goes?

(*Exit* Tranto, *back* .)

MISS STARKEY. Forty minutes.

CULVER. Excellent.

MISS STARKEY (*indicating some papers which she has brought*). These things ought to be attended to to-night.

CULVER. Possibly. But they won't be.

MISS STARKEY. The Rosenberg matter is very urgent. He leaves for Glasgow to-morrow.

CULVER. I wish he'd leave for Berlin. I won't touch it to-night. Please take down these two letters.

MISS STARKEY. Then it will be necessary for you to be at the office at 9.30 in the morning.

CULVER. I decline to be at the office at 9.30 in the morning.

MISS STARKEY. But I've an appointment for you. I was afraid you wouldn't do anything to-night.

CULVER (*resigned*). Very well! Very well! Tell them to call me, and see cook about breakfast. (*Beginning to dictate* .) 'My dear Lord Woking'—

MISS STARKEY (*sitting*). Excuse me, is this letter about the title?

CULVER. Yes.

MISS STARKEY. Then it ought to be an autograph letter. That's the etiquette.

CULVER. How do you know?

MISS STARKEY. General knowledge.

CULVER. In this case the rule will be broken. That's flat.

MISS STARKEY. Then I must imitate your handwriting.

CULVER. Can you?

MISS STARKEY. You ought to know, Mr. Culver—by this time.

CULVER. I don't know officially. However, have your own way. Forge the whole thing, signature and all. I don't care. 'My dear Lord Woking. Extreme pressure of—er—government business has compelled me to leave till last thing to-night my reply to your letter in which you are good enough to

38

communicate to me the offer of a baronetcy. I cannot adequately express to you my sense of the honour in contemplation, but, comma, for certain personal reasons with which I need not trouble you, comma, I feel bound, with the greatest respect and the greatest gratitude, to ask to be allowed to refuse. (Miss Starkey *shows emotion* .) I am sure I can rely on you to convey my decision to the proper quarter with all your usual tact. Believe me, my dear Lord Woking, Cordially yours.' (*To* Miss Starkey.) What in heaven's name is the matter with you?

MISS STARKEY. Mr. Culver. I shall have to give you a month's notice.

CULVER (*staggered*). Have—have you gone mad too?

MISS STARKEY. Not that I am aware of. But I must give a month's notice— for certain personal reasons with which I need not trouble you. CULVER. Young woman, you know that you are absolutely indispensable to me. You know that without you I should practically cease to exist. I am quite open with you as to that—and as to everything. You are acquainted with the very depths of my character and the most horrible secrets of my life. I conceal nothing from you, and I demand that you conceal nothing from me. What are your reasons for giving me notice in this manner?

MISS STARKEY. My self respect would not allow me to remain with a gentleman who had refused a title. Oh, Mr. Culver, to be the private secretary to a baronet has been my life's dream. And—and—I have just had the offer of a place where a *peerage* is in prospect. Still, I wouldn't have, taken even that if you had not—if you had not—(*controlling herself, coldly*). Kindly accept my notice. I give it at once because I shall have no time to lose for the peerage.

CULVER. Miss Starkey, you drive me to the old, old conclusion—all women are alike.

MISS STARKEY. Then my leaving will cause you no inconvenience, because you'll easily get another girl exactly like me.

CULVER. You are a heartless creature. (*In an ordinary voice* .) Did we finish the first letter? This is the second one. (*Dictates* .) 'My dear Lord Woking'—

MISS STARKEY. But you've just given me that one.

CULVER (*firmly* .) 'My dear Lord Woking.' Go on the same as the first one down to 'I cannot adequately express to you my sense of the honour in contemplation.' 'Full stop. I need hardly say that, in spite of my feeling that I have done only too little to deserve it, I accept it with the greatest pleasure and the greatest gratitude. Believe me, etc.'

MISS STARKEY. But—

CULVER. Don't imagine that your giving me notice has affected me in the slightest degree. It has not. I told you I had two letters. I have not yet decided whether to accept or refuse the title. (*Enter* Mrs. Culver, *back* .) Go and copy both letters and bring them in to me in a quarter of an hour, whether I ring or not. That will give you plenty of time for post. Now—run! (*Exit* Miss Starkey, *back* . Culver *rises, clears his throat, and obviously braces himself for a final effort of firmness* . Mrs. Culver *calmly rearranges some flowers in a vase* .) Well, my dear, I was expecting you.

MRS. CULVER (*very sweetly*), Arthur, I was wrong.

CULVER (*startled*). Good God! (Mrs. Culver *bends down to examine the upholstery of a chair* . Culver *gives a gesture, first of triumph, and then of apprehension* .)

MRS. CULVER (*looking straight at him*). I say I was wrong.

CULVER (*lightly, but uneasily*). Oh no! Oh no!

MRS. CULVER. Of course I don't mean wrong in my arguments about the title. Not for a moment. I mean I was wrong not to sacrifice my own point of view. I'm only a woman, and it's the woman's place to submit. So I do submit. Naturally I shall always be a true wife to you, but—

CULVER. Now child, don't begin to talk like that. I don't mind *reading* novels, but I won't have raw lumps of them thrown *at* me.

MRS. CULVER (*with a gentle smile*), I *must* talk like this. I shall do everything I can to make you comfortable, and I hope nobody, and especially not the poor children, will notice any difference in our relations.

CULVER (*advancing, with a sort of menace*). But?

MRS. CULVER. But things can never be the same again.

CULVER. I knew the confounded phrase was coming. I knew it. I've read it scores of times. (*Picking up the vase* .) Hermione, if you continue in that strain, I will dash this vase into a thousand fragments.

MRS. CULVER (*quietly taking the vase from him and putting it down*). Arthur, I could have forgiven you everything. What do I care—really—about a title? (*Falsely* .) I only care for your happiness. But I can't forgive you for having laid a trap for me last night—and in front of the children and a stranger too.

CULVER. Laid a trap for you?

MRS. CULVER. You knew all about the title when you first came in last night and you deliberately led me on.

CULVER. Oh! That! Ah well! One does what one can. You've laid many a trap for me, my girl. You're still about ten up and two to play in the trap game.

MRS. CULVER. I've never laid a trap for you.

CULVER. Fibster! Come here. (Mrs. Culver *hesitates* .) Come hither—and be kissed. (*She approaches submissively, and then, standing like a marble statue, allows herself to be kissed* . Culver *assumes the attitude of the triumphant magnanimous male* .) There! That's all right.

MRS. CULVER (*having moved away; still very sweetly and coldly*). Can I do anything else for you before I go to bed?

CULVER (*ignoring the question; grandly and tolerantly*). Do you suppose, my marble statue, that after all I've said at the Club about the rascality of this Honours business, I could ever have appeared there as a New Year Baronet? The thing's unthinkable. Why, I should have had to resign and join another Club!

MRS. CULVER (*calmly and severely*). So that's it, is it? I might have known what was really at the bottom of it all. Your Club again! You have to choose between your wife and your Club, and of course it's your wife that must suffer. Naturally!

CULVER. Go on! You'll be saying next that I've committed bigamy with my Club.

MRS. CULVER (*with youthful vivacity*). I'm an old woman—

CULVER (*flatteringly*). Yes, look at you! Hag! When I fell in love with you your hair was still down. The marvel to me is that I ever let you put it up.

MRS. CULVER. I'm only an old woman now. You have had the best part of my life. You might have given me great pleasure with this title. But no! Your Club comes first. And what a child you are! As if there's one single member of your Club who wouldn't envy you your baronetcy! However, I've nothing more to say. (*Moving towards the door, back* .) Oh yes, I have. (*Casually* .) I've decided to go away to-morrow and stay with grandma for a long holiday. She needs me, and if I'm not to break down entirely I must have a change. I've told Hildegarde our—arrangements. The poor girl's terribly upset. Please don't disturb me in the morning. I shall take the noon train. Good-night.

CULVER. Hermione!

MRS. CULVER (*returning a little from the direction of the door, submissively*). Yes, Arthur.

CULVER. If you keep on playing the martyr much longer there will be bloodshed, and you'll know what martyrdom is.

MRS. CULVER (*in a slightly relenting tone*). Arthur, you were always conscientious. Your conscience is working.

CULVER. I have no conscience. Never had.

MRS. CULVER (*persuasively, and with much charm*). Yes you have, and it's urging you to give way to your sensible little wife. You know you're only bluffing.

CULVER. Indeed I'm not.

MRS. CULVER. Yes, you are. Mr. Tranto advised you to give way, and you think such a lot of his opinion.

CULVER. Who told you Tranto advised me to give way?

MRS. CULVER. He did.

CULVER. Damn him!

MRS. CULVER (*soothingly*). Yes, yes.

CULVER. No, no!

MRS. CULVER. And your dear, indispensable Miss Starkey thinks the same. (*She tries to kiss him* .) CULVER. No, no! (Mrs. Culver *succeeds in kissing him* .)

Enter Miss Starkey.

(*The other two spring apart. A short pause* .)

CULVER. Which is the refusal?

MISS STARKEY. This one.

CULVER. Put it in the fire. (Miss Starkey *obeys. Both the women show satisfaction in their different ways* .) Give me the acceptance. (*He takes the letter of acceptance and reads it* .)

MRS. CULVER (*while he is reading the letter*). Miss Starkey, you look very pale. Have you had any dinner?

MISS STARKEY. Not yet, madam.

MRS. CULVER. You poor dear! (*She strokes* Miss Starkey. *They both look at the tyrannical male* .) I'll order something for you at once.

MISS STARKEY. I shall have to go to the post first.

42

CULVER (*glancing up*). I'll go to the post myself. I must have air, air! Where's the envelope? (*Exit* Miss Starkey *quickly, back* .) (Mrs. Culver *gently takes the letter from her husband and reads it* . Culver *drops into a chair* .)

MRS. CULVER (*putting down the letter*). Darling!

CULVER. I thought I was a brute?

MRS. CULVER (*caressing and kissing him*). I do so love my brute, and I am so happy. Darling! But you are a silly old darling, wasting all this time.

CULVER. Wasting all what time?

MRS. CULVER. Why, the moment I came in again I could see you'd decided to give way. (*With a gesture of delight* .) I must run and tell the children. (*Exit, L* .)

Enter Miss Starkey *back* .

MISS STARKEY. Here's the envelope.

CULVER (*taking it*). Tell them to get me my hat and overcoat.

MISS STARKEY. Yes, Sir Arthur. (Culver *starts* .) (*Exit* Miss Starkey, *back* .)

CULVER (*as he puts the letter in the envelope; with an air of discovery*). I suppose I *do* like being called 'Sir Arthur.'

Enter Hildegard *and* John *both disgusted, back* .

JOHN (*to* Hildegarde, *as they come in*). I told you last night he couldn't control even the mater. However, I'll be even with her yet.

CULVER. What do you mean, boy?

JOHN. I mean I'll be even with the mater yet. You'll see.

HILDEGARDE. Papa, you've behaved basely. Basely! What an example to us! I intend to leave this house and live alone.

CULVER. You ought to marry Mr. Sampson Straight. (Hildegarde *starts and is silent* .)

JOHN. Fancy me having to go back to school the son of a rotten baronet, and with the frightful doom of being a rotten baronet myself. What price the anti-hereditary-principle candidate! Dad, I hope you won't die just yet—it would ruin my political career. Stay me with flagons!

CULVER. Me too!

CURTAIN.

ACT III

ACT III

The next day, before lunch . Hildegarde *and* John *are together* .

JOHN (*nervously impatient*). I wish she'd come.

HILDEGARDE. She'll be here in a moment. She's fussing round dad.

JOHN. Is he really ill?

HILDEGARDE. Well of course. It came on in the night, after he'd had time to think things over. Why?

JOHN. I read in some paper about the Prime Minister having only a *political* chill. So I thought perhaps the pater—under the circs—

HILDEGARDE (*shaking her head*). You can't have political dyspepsia. Can't fake the symptoms. Who is to begin this affair, you or me?

JOHN. Depends. What line are you going on with her?

HILDEGARDE. I'm going to treat her exactly as she treats me. I've just thought of it. Only I shan't lose my temper.

JOHN. Sugarsticks?

HILDEGARDE. Yes.

JOHN. You'll never be able to keep it up.

HILDEGARDE. O yes I shall. Somehow I feel much more mature than I did yesterday.

JOHN. More mature? Stay me with flagons! I was always mature. If you knew what rot I think school is…! Well, anyway, you can begin.

HILDEGARDE. You're very polite to-day, Johnnie.

JOHN. Don't mention it. My argument 'll be the best, and I want to keep it for the end, that's all.

HILDEGARDE. Thanks. But I bet you we shall both fail.

JOHN. Well, if we do, I've still got something else waiting for her ladyship. A regular startler, my child.

HILDEGARDE. What is it?

Enter Mrs. Culver, *back* .

46

JOHN (*to* Hildegarde, *as* Mrs. Culver *enters*). Wait and see.

MRS. CULVER (*cheerful and affectionate, to* John). So you've come in. (*To* Hildegarde.) You *are* back early to-day! Well, my darlings, what do you want me for?

HILDEGARDE (*imitating her mothers manner*). Well, mamma darling, we hate bothering you. We know you've got quite enough worries, without having any more. But it's about this baronetcy business. (Mrs. Culver *starts* .) Do be an angel and listen to us.

MRS. CULVER (*with admirable self-control*). Of course, my pet. But you know the matter is quite, quite settled. Your father and I settled it together last night, and the letter of acceptance is in the hands of the Government by this time.

JOHN. It isn't, mater. It's here. (*Pulls the letter out of his pocket* .)

MRS. CULVER. John! What—

JOHN. Now, now, mater! Keep calm. This is really your own doing. Pater wanted to go to the post himself, but it was raining a bit, and you're always in such a fidget about his getting his feet wet you wouldn't let him go, and so I went instead.

HILDEGARDE. Yes, mummy darling, you must acknowledge that you were putting temptation in Johnnie's way.

JOHN. Soon as I got outside, I said to myself: 'I think the pater ought to have a night to think over this affair. It's very important. And he can easily send round an answer by hand in the morning.' So I didn't post the letter. I should have told you earlier, but you weren't down for breakfast, and I had to go out afterwards on urgent private business.

MRS. CULVER. But—but—(*Controlling herself, grieved, but kind* .) Your father will be terribly angry. I daren't face him.

JOHN (*only half-suppressing his amusement at the last remark*). Don't let that worry you. I'll face him. He'll be delighted. He'll write another letter, and quite a different one.

MRS. CULVER (*getting firmer*). But don't I tell you, my dearest boy, that the affair is settled, quite settled?

JOHN. It isn't settled so long as I've got this letter, anyway.

HILDEGARDE. Of course it isn't settled. Mother darling, we simply must look the facts in the face. Fact one, the letter is here. Fact two, the whole family is most frightfully upset. Dad's ill—

MRS. CULVER. That was the lobster.

JOHN. It wasn't.

MRS. CULVER. Yes, dear. Lobster always upsets him.

JOHN. It didn't this time.

MRS. CULVER. How do you know?

JOHN. I know, because *I* ate all his lobster. He shoved it over to me. You couldn't see for the fruit-bowl.

HILDEGARDE. No, mamma sweetest. It's this baronetcy business that's knocked poor papa over. And it's knocked over Johnnie and me too. I'm perfectly, perfectly sure you acted for the best, but don't you think you persuaded father against his judgment? Not to speak of our judgment!

MRS. CULVER. I've only one thought—

HILDEGARDE (*caressing and kissing her mother*). I know! I know! Father's happiness. Our happiness. Mamma, please don't imagine for a single instant that we don't realise that. You're the most delicious darling of an old mater—

MRS. CULVER (*slightly suspicious*). Hildegarde, you're quite a different girl to-day.

HILDEGARDE (*nods*). I've aged in a single night. I've become ever so serious. This baronetcy business has shown me that I've got convictions—and deep convictions. I admit I'm a different girl to-day. But then everything's different to-day. The whole house is different. Johnnie's different. Papa's missed going to the office for the first time in eight months. (*Very sweetly* .) Surely you must see, mamma, that something ought to be done, and that you alone can do it.

MRS. CULVER. What? What ought I to do?

HILDEGARDE. Go upstairs and tell dad you've changed your mind about the title, and advise him to write off instantly and refuse it. You know you always twist him round your little finger.

MRS. CULVER (*looking at her little finger*). I shouldn't dream of trying to influence your father once he had decided. And he *has* decided.

HILDEGARDE (*sweetly*). Mamma, you're most tremendously clever—far cleverer than any of us—but I'm not sure if you understand the attitude of the modern girl towards things that affect her convictions.

MRS. CULVER (*sweetly*). Are you the modern girl?

HILDEGARDE. Yes.

MRS. CULVER. Well, I'm the ancient girl. And I can tell you this—you're very like me, and we're both very like somebody else.

HILDEGARDE. Who's that.

MRS. CULVER. Eve.

JOHN. Come, mater. Eve would never have learnt typewriting. She'd have gone on the land.

MRS. CULVER. John, your sister and I are not jesting.

HILDEGARDE. I'm so glad you admit I'm serious, mamma. Because I am— very. I don't want to threaten—

MRS. CULVER. Threaten, darling?

HILDEGARDE (*firmly, but quite lightly and sweetly*). No, darling. *Not* to threaten. The mere idea of threatening is absurd. But it would be extremely unfair to you not to tell you that unless you agree to father refusing the title, I shall have to leave the house and live by myself. I really shall. Of course I can easily earn my own living. I quite see that you have principles. But I also have principles. If they clash—naturally it's my place to retire. And I shall, mamma dearest.

MRS. CULVER. Is that final?

HILDEGARDE. Final, mummy darling.

MRS. CULVER. Then, my dearest child, you must go.

HILDEGARDE (*still sweetly*). Is that final?

MRS. CULVER (*still sweetly*). Final, my poor pet.

JOHN (*firmly*). Now let *me* say a word.

MRS. CULVER (*benignly*). And what have you got to say in the matter? You've already been very naughty about that letter. Do try not to be ridiculous. Give me the letter. This affair has nothing to do with you. JOHN (*putting the letter in his pocket*). Nothing whatever to do with me! Mater, you really are a bit too thick. If it was a knighthood, I wouldn't care. You could have your blooming knighthood. Knighthoods do come to an end. Baronetcies go on for ever. I've told the dad, and I'll tell you, that *I will not have* my political career ruined by any baronetcy. And if you insist—may I respectfully inform you what I shall do? May I respectfully inform you—may I?

MRS. CULVER. John!

JOHN. I shall chuck Siege and go into the Flying Corps. And that's flat. If you really want to shorten my life, all you have to do is to stick to that bally baronetcy.

MRS. CULVER. Your father won't allow you to join the Flying Corps.

JOHN. My father can't stop me. I know the mess is expensive, but the pay's good, and I've got £150 of my own. Not a fortune! Not a fortune! But enough, quite enough. *A short life and a merry one* . I went to see Captain Skewes at the Automobile this morning. One of our old boys. He's delighted. He gave me Lanchester's 'Aircraft in Warfare' to read. Here it is. (*Picking up the book* .) Here it *is* ! I shall be sitting up all night to-night reading it. *A short life and a merry one* .

MRS. CULVER. You don't mean it!

JOHN. I absolutely do.

MRS. CULVER (*after a pause*). John, you're trying to bully your mother.

JOHN. Not in the least, mater. I'm merely telling you what will happen if father accepts that piffling baronetcy.

MRS. CULVER (*checking a tear; very sweetly*). Well, my pets, you make life just a little difficult for me. I live only for you and your father. I think first of your father, and then of you two. For myself, I am perfectly indifferent. I consider all politics extremely silly. There never were any in my family, nor in your father's. And to me it's most extraordinary that your father should catch them so late in life. I always supposed that after thirty people were immune. (*To* John.) You, I suppose, were bound to have them sooner or later, but that *Hilda* should go out of her way to contract them—well, it passes me. It passes me. However, I've no more to say. Your father had made up his mind to accept the title. You want him to refuse it. I hate to influence him (Hildegarde *again hides a cynical smile*) but for your sakes I'll try to persuade him to alter his decision and refuse it.

JOHN (*taking her arm*). Come along then—now! I'll go with you to see fair play. (*He opens the door, L, and* Mrs. Culver *passes out. Then stopping in the doorway, to* Hildegarde) Who did the trick? I say—who did the trick?

HILDEGARDE (*nicely*). Pooh! You may be a prefect at school. But here you're only mamma's wee lamb! (*She drops on to the sofa* .)

JOHN (*singing triumphantly*). Stay—me—with fla—gons! (*Exit John, L* .)

       Enter Tranto, *back, shown in by the* Parlourmaid.

TRANTO. How d'ye do, Miss Hilda. I'm in a high state of nerves.

HILDEGARDE (*shaking hands weakly*). We all are.

TRANTO (*ignoring what she says*). I've come specially to see you.

HILDEGARDE. But how did you know I should be here—at this time? I'm supposed to be at the Food Ministry till one o'clock?

TRANTO. I called for you at the Ministry.

HILDEGARDE (*leaning forward*). That's quite against the rules. The rules are made for the moral protection of the women-clerks.

TRANTO. They told me you'd left early.

HILDEGARDE. Why did you call?

TRANTO. Shall I be frank?

HILDEGARDE. Are you ever?

TRANTO. I wanted to walk home with you.

HILDEGARDE. Are you getting frightened about that next article of mine?

TRANTO. No. I've lost all interest in articles.

HILDEGARDE. Even in my articles?

TRANTO. Even in yours. I'm only interested in the writer of your articles. (*Agitated* .) Miss Hilda, the hour is about to strike.

HILDEGARDE. What hour?

TRANTO. Listen, please. Let me explain. The situation is this. Instinct has got hold of me. When I woke up this morning something inside me said: 'You must call at the Ministry for that young woman and walk home with her.' This idea seemed marvellously beautiful to me; it seemed one of the most enchanting ideas that had ever entered the heart of man. I thought of nothing else all the morning. When I reached the Ministry and you'd gone, I felt as if I'd been shot. Then I rushed here. If you hadn't been at home I don't know what I should have done. My fever has been growing every moment. Providentially you *are* here. I give you fair warning that I'm utterly in the grip of an instinct which is ridiculously unconventional and which will brook no delay. I repeat, the hour is about to strike.

HILDEGARDE (*rousing herself*). Before it actually strikes, I want to ask a question.

TRANTO. But that's just what *I* want to do.

HILDEGARDE. Please. One moment of your valuable time.

TRANTO. The whole of my life.

HILDEGARDE. Last night, why did you advise papa to give way to mamma and accept the baronetcy?

TRANTO. Did I?

HILDEGARDE. It seems so.

TRANTO. Well—er—

HILDEGARDE. You know it's quite against his principles, and against mine and Johnnie's, not to speak of yours.

TRANTO. The fact is, you yourself had given me such an account of your mother's personality that I felt sure she'd win anyhow; and—and—for reasons of my own, I wished to be on the winning side. No harm in that, surely. And as regards principles, I have a theory about principles. Your father was much struck by it when I told him.

HILDEGARDE. Namely?

TRANTO. There are no principles in married life.

HILDEGARDE. Oh, indeed! Well, there may not be any principles in your married life, but there most positively will be in mine, if I ever have a married life. And let me tell you that you aren't on the winning side after all—you're on the losing side.

TRANTO. How? Has your—

HILDEGARDE. Johnnie and I have had a great interview with mamma, and she's yielded. She's abandoned the baronetcy. In half an hour from now the baronetcy will have been definitely and finally refused.

TRANTO. Great Scott!

HILDEGARDE. You're startled?

TRANTO. No! After all, I might have foreseen that you'd come out on top. The day before yesterday your modesty was making you say that your mother could eat you. I, on the contrary, insisted that you could eat your mother. Who was right? I ask: who was right? When it really comes to the point—well, you have a serious talk with your mother, and she gives in!

HILDEGARDE (*gloomily*). No! *I* didn't do it. I tried, and failed. Then Johnnie tried, and did it without the slightest trouble. A schoolboy! That's why I'm so upset.

TRANTO (*shaking his head*). You musn't tell me that, Miss Hilda. Of course it was you that did it.

HILDEGARDE (*impatiently; standing up*). But I *do* tell you.

TRANTO. Sorry! Sorry! Do be merciful! My feelings about you at this very moment are so, if I may use the term, unbridled—

HILDEGARDE (*with false gentle calm*). And that's not all. I suppose you haven't by any chance told father that I'm Sampson Straight?

TRANTO. Certainly not.

HILDEGARDE. You're sure?

TRANTO. Absolutely.

HILDEGARDE. Well, I'm sorry.

TRANTO. Why?

HILDEGARDE (*quietly sarcastic*). Because papa told me you did tell him. Therefore father is a liar. I don't like being the daughter of a liar. I hate liars.

TRANTO. Aren't you rather cutting yourself off from mankind?

HILDEGARDE (*going straight on*). For the last day or two father had been giving me such queer little digs every now and then that I began to suspect he knew who Sampson Straight was. So I asked him right out this morning—he was in bed—and he had to acknowledge he did know and that you told him.

TRANTO. Well, I didn't exactly tell him. He sort of guessed, and I—

HILDEGARDE (*calmly, relentlessly*). You told him.

TRANTO. No. I merely admitted it. You think I ought to have denied it?

HILDEGARDE. Of course you ought to have denied it.

TRANTO. But it was true.

HILDEGARDE. And if it was?

TRANTO. If it was true, how could I deny it? You've just said you hate liars.

HILDEGARDE (*losing self-control*). Please don't be absurd.

TRANTO (*a little nettled*). I apologise.

HILDEGARDE. What for?

TRANTO. For having put you in the wrong. It's such shocking bad diplomacy for any man to put any woman in the wrong.

HILDEGARDE (*angrily*). Man—woman! Man—woman! There you are! It's always the same with you males. Sex! Sex! Sex!

TRANTO (*quite conquering his annoyance; persuasively*). But I'm fatally in love with you. HILDEGARDE. Well, of course there you have the advantage of me.

TRANTO. Don't you care a little—

HILDEGARDE (*letting herself go*). Why should I care? What have I done to make you imagine I care? It's quite true that I've saved your newspaper from an early grave. It was suffering from rickets, spinal curvature, and softening of the brain; and I've performed a miraculous cure on it with my articles. I'm Sampson Straight. But that's not enough for you. You can't keep sentiment out of business. No man ever could. You'd like Sampson Straight to wear blouses and bracelets for you, and loll on sofas for you, and generally offer you the glad eye. It's an insult. And then on the top of all, you go and give the whole show away to papa, in spite of our understanding; and if papa hadn't been the greatest dear in the world you might have got me into the most serious difficulties.

TRANTO (*equably, after a pause*), I don't think I'll ask myself to stay for lunch.

HILDEGARDE. Good morning.

TRANTO (*near the door*). I suppose I'd better announce that he's died very suddenly under mysterious circumstances?

HILDEGARDE. Who?

TRANTO. Sampson Straight.

HILDEGARDE. And what about my new article, that you've got in hand?

TRANTO. It can be a posthumous article, in a black border.

HILDEGARDE. Indeed! And why shouldn't Sampson Straight transfer his services to another paper? There are several who'd jump at him.

TRANTO. I never thought of that.

HILDEGARDE. Naturally!

TRANTO. He shall live.

(*A pause* . Tranto *bows, and exit, back* .)

(Hildegarde *subsides once more on to the sofa* .)

Enter Culver, *in his velvet coat, L* .

CULVER (*softly, with sprightliness*). Hello, Sampson!

HILDEGARDE. Dad, please don't call me that.

CULVER. Not when we're alone? Why?

HILDEGARDE. I—I—Dad, I'm in a fearful state of nerves just now. Lost my temper and all sorts of calamities.

CULVER. Really! I'd no idea. I gathered that the interview between you and your mother had passed quite smoothly.

HILDEGARDE. Oh! *That!*

CULVER. What do you mean—'Oh! *That!* '?

HILDEGARDE (*standing; in a new, less gloomy tone*). Papa, what are you doing out of bed? You're very ill.

CULVER. Well, I'd managed to dress before your mother and Johnnie came. As soon as they imparted to me the glad tidings that baronetcies were off I felt so well I decided to come down and thank you for your successful efforts on behalf of the family well-being. I'm no longer your father. I'm your brother.

HILDEGARDE. It was Johnnie did it.

CULVER. It wasn't— *I* know.

HILDEGARDE (*exasperated*). I say it *was!* (*Apologetically*). So sorry, dad. (*Kisses him*). Where are they, those two? (*Sits*). CULVER. Mother and John? Don't know. I fancy somebody called as I came down.

HILDEGARDE. Called! Before lunch! Who was it?

CULVER. Haven't the faintest.

Enter John, *back* .

JOHN (*proudly*). I say, good people! New acquaintance of mine! Just looked in. Met him at the Automobile this morning with Skewes. I was sure you'd all give your heads to see the old chap, so I asked him to lunch on the chance. Dashed if he didn't accept! You see we'd been talking a bit about politics. He's the most celebrated man in London. I doubt if there's a fellow I admire more in the whole world—or you either. He's knocked the mater flat already. Between ourselves, I really asked him because I thought he might influence her on this baronetcy business. However, that's all off now. What are you staring at?

CULVER. We're only bursting with curiosity to hear the name of this paragon of yours. As a general rule I like to know beforehand whom I'm going to lunch with in my own house.

JOHN. It's Sampson Straight.

HILDEGARDE (*springing up*). *Sampson Str* —

55

CULVER (*calmly*). Keep your nerve, Hilda. Keep your nerve.

JOHN. I thought I wouldn't say anything till he'd actually arrived. He mightn't have come at all. Then what a fool I should have looked if I'd told you he *was* coming! Tranto himself doesn't know him. Tranto pooh-poohed the idea of me ever meeting him, Tranto did. Well, I've met him, and he's here. I haven't let on to him that I know Tranto. I'm going to bring them together and watch them both having the surprise of their lives.

CULVER. John, this is a great score for you. I admit I've never been more interested in meeting anyone. Never!

Enter Parlourmaid, *back* .

PARLOURMAID. Miss Starkey, sir.

CULVER (*cheerfully*). I'll see her soon. (*Pulling himself up suddenly; in an alarmed, gloomy tone* .) No, no! I can't possibly see her.

PARLOURMAID. Miss Starkey says there are several important letters, sir.

CULVER. No, no! I'm not equal to it.

HILDEGARDE (*confidentially*). What's wrong, dad?

CULVER (*to* Hildegarde). She'll give me notice the minute she knows she can't call me Sir Arthur. (*Shudders* .) I quail.

Enter Mrs. Culver *and* Sampson Straight, *back* .

(*The* Parlourmaid *holds the door for them, and then exit* .)

MRS. CULVER. This is my husband. Arthur, dear—Mr. Sampson Straight. And this is my little daughter. (Hilda *bows* , John *surveys the scene with satisfaction* .)

CULVER (*recovering his equipoise; shaking hands heartily*). Mr. Straight. Delighted to meet you. I simply cannot tell you how unexpected this pleasure is.

STRAIGHT. You're too kind.

CULVER (*gaily*). I doubt it. I doubt it.

STRAIGHT. I ought to apologise for coming in like this. But I've been so charmingly received by Mrs. Culver—

MRS. CULVER. You've been so charming about my boy, Mr. Straight.
STRAIGHT. I was so very greatly impressed by your son this morning at the Club that I couldn't resist the opportunity he gave me of visiting his home.

What I say is: like parents, like child. I'm an old-fashioned man.

MRS. CULVER. No one would guess that from your articles in *The Echo* . Of course they're frightfully clever, but you know I don't quite agree with all your opinions.

STRAIGHT. Neither do I. You see—there's always a difference between what one thinks and what one has to write.

MRS. CULVER. I'm so glad. (Culver *starts and looks round* .) What is it, Arthur?

CULVER. Nothing! I thought I heard the ice cracking. (Hildegarde *begins to smile* .)

STRAIGHT (*looking at the floor; simply*). Ice?

MRS. CULVER. Arthur!

STRAIGHT. It was still thawing when I came in. As I was saying, I'm an old-fashioned man. And I'm a provincial—and proud of it.

MRS. CULVER. But my dear Mr. Straight, really, if you'll excuse me, you look as if you never left the pavement of Piccadilly. CULVER. Say the windows of the Turf club, darling.

STRAIGHT (*serenely*). No. I live very, very quietly on my little place, and when I feel the need of contact with the great world I run over for the afternoon to—St. Ives.

MRS. CULVER. How remarkable! Then that explains how it is you're so deliciously unspoilt.

STRAIGHT. Do you mean my face?

MRS. CULVER. I meant you don't seem at all to realise that you're a very great celebrity in London; very great indeed. A lion of the first order.

STRAIGHT (*simply*). Lion?

CULVER. You're expected to roar, Mr. Straight.

STRAIGHT. Roar?

MRS. CULVER. It may interest you to know that my little daughter also writes articles in *The Echo* . Yes, about war cookery. But of course you wouldn't notice them. (Hildegarde *moves away* .) I'm afraid (*apologetically*) your mere presence is making her just a wee bit nervous. HILDEGARDE (*from a distance, striving to control herself*). Oh, Mr. Sampson Straight. There's one question I've been longing to ask you. I always ask it of literary lions—and tigers.

STRAIGHT. Tigers?

HILDEGARDE. Do you write best in the morning or do you burn the midnight oil?

STRAIGHT. Oil?

MRS. CULVER. Do sit down, Mr. Straight. (*She goes imploringly to* Hildegarde, *who has lost control of herself and is getting a little hysterical with mirth. Aside to* Hildegarde.) Hilda! (John, *puzzled and threatening, also approaches* Hildegarde.)

CULVER (*sitting down by* Straight.) And so, although you prefer a country life, the lure of London has been too strong for you in the end.

STRAIGHT. I came to town on business.

CULVER. Ah!

STRAIGHT. The fact is, business of the utmost importance. Perhaps I may be able to interest you in it.

CULVER. Now we're getting hotter.

STRAIGHT. Hotter?

CULVER. Go on, go on, Mr. Straight.

STRAIGHT. To tell you the truth—

CULVER. Always a wise thing to do.

STRAIGHT. One of my reasons for accepting your son's kind invitation was that I thought that conceivably you might be willing to help in a great patriotic scheme of mine. Naturally you show surprise.

CULVER. Do I? Then I'm expressing myself badly. I'm not in the least surprised. It is the contrary that would have surprised me.

STRAIGHT. We may possibly discuss it later.

CULVER. Later? Why later? Why not at once? I'm full of curiosity. I hate to let the grass grow under my feet.

STRAIGHT (*looking at the floor*). Grass? (*With a faint mechanical laugh* .) Ah yes, I see. Figure of speech. Well, I'm starting a little limited liability syndicate.

CULVER. Precisely what I thought. Yes?

STRAIGHT. The End-the-war Syndicate.

JOHN (*approaching*). But surely you aren't one of those pacifists, Mr.

Straight! You've always preached fighting it out to a finish.

STRAIGHT. The object of my syndicate is certainly to fight to a finish, but to finish in about a week—by means of my little syndicate.

CULVER. Splendid! But there is one draw-back. New capital issues are forbidden under the Defence of the Realm Act.

STRAIGHT. Even when the object is to win the war?

CULVER. My dear sir, the Treasury would never permit such a thing.

STRAIGHT. Well, we needn't have a limited company. Perhaps after all it would be better to keep it quite private.

CULVER. Oh! It would. And what is the central idea of this charming syndicate?

STRAIGHT. The idea is—(*looking round cautiously*)—a new explosive.

CULVER. Again, precisely what I thought. Your own invention?

STRAIGHT. No. A friend of mine. It truly is the most marvellous explosive.

CULVER. I suppose it bangs everything.

STRAIGHT (*simply*). Oh, it does. A development of trinitrotoluol on new lines. I needn't say that my interest in the affair is purely patriotic.

CULVER. Of course. Of course.

STRAIGHT. I can easily get all the capital I need.

CULVER. Of course. Of course.

STRAIGHT. But I'm not in close touch with the official world, and in a matter of this kind official influence is absolutely essential to success. Now you *are* in touch with the official world. I shouldn't ask you to subscribe, though if you cared to do so there would be no objection. And I may say that the syndicate can't help making a tremendous lot of money. When I tell you that the new explosive is forty-seven times as powerful as trinitrotoluol itself —

CULVER. When you tell me that, Mr. Straight, I can only murmur the hope that you haven't got any of it in your pocket.

STRAIGHT (*simply*). Oh, no! Please don't be alarmed. But you see the immense possibilities. You see how this explosive would end the war practically at once. And you'll understand, of course, that although my articles in *The Echo* have apparently caused considerable commotion in London, and given me a position which I am glad to be able to use for the service of the Empire, my interest in mere journalism as such has almost ceased since my friend asked me to be secretary and treasurer of the syndicate.

CULVER. And so you're the secretary *and* treasurer?

STRAIGHT. Yes. We don't want to have subscribers of less than £100 each. If you cared to look into the matter—I know you're very busy, but a mere glance—

CULVER. Just so—a mere glance.

Enter Tranto *excitedly* .

HILDEGARDE (*nearer the door than the rest*). Again?

TRANTO (*rather loudly and not specially to* Hildegarde). Terrible news! I've just heard and I rushed back to tell you. Sampson Straight has died very suddenly in Cornwall. Bright's disease. He breathed his last in his own potato patch. (*Aside to* Hildegarde, *in response to a gesture from her*) I'm awfully sorry. The poor fellow simply had to expire.

MRS. CULVER (*to* Tranto). Now this just shows how the most absurd rumours *do* get abroad! Here *is* Mr. Sampson Straight. I'm *so* glad you've come, because you've always wanted to meet him in the flesh.

TRANTO (*to* Straight). Are you Sampson Straight?

STRAIGHT. I am, sir.

TRANTO. The Sampson Straight who lives in Cornwall?

STRAIGHT. Just so.

TRANTO. Impossible!

STRAIGHT. Pardon me. One moment. I was told there was a danger of my being inconvenienced in London by one of these military raids for rounding up slackers, and as I happen to have a rather youthful appearance, I took the precaution of bringing with me my birth-certificate and registration card. (*Produces them* .)

TRANTO (*glancing at the card*). And it's really you who write those brilliant articles in *The Echo* ?

STRAIGHT. 'Brilliant'—I won't say. But I do write them.

TRANTO. Well, this is the most remarkable instance of survival after death that I ever came across.

STRAIGHT. I beg your pardon.

TRANTO. You're dead, my fine fellow. Your place isn't here. You ought to be in the next world. You're a humbug.

STRAIGHT (*to* Mrs. Culver). I'm not quite sure that I understand. Will you kindly introduce me?

MRS. CULVER. I'm so sorry. This is Mr. Tranto, proprietor and editor of *The Echo* —(*apologetically, with an uneasy smile*) a great humourist.

STRAIGHT (*thunderstruck; aside*). Well, I'm damned! (*His whole demeanour changes. Nevertheless, while tacitly admitting that he is found out, he at once resumes his mild calmness. To* Culver.) I've just remembered an appointment of vital importance. I'm afraid our little talk about the syndicate must be adjourned.

CULVER. I feared you might have to hurry away.

(Straight *bows as a preliminary to departure* .)

(John, *deeply humiliated, averts his glance from everybody* .)

TRANTO. Here! But you can't go off like this.

STRAIGHT. Why? Have you anything against me?

TRANTO. Nothing (*casually*) except that you're an impostor.

STRAIGHT. I fail to see it.

TRANTO. But haven't you just said that you write those articles in my paper?

STRAIGHT. Oh! *That* ! Well, of course, if I'd known who you were I shouldn't have dreamed of saying any such thing. I always try to suit my talk to my company.

TRANTO. This time you didn't quite bring it off.

STRAIGHT. Perhaps I owe you some slight explanation (*looking round blandly*).

CULVER. Do you really think so?

STRAIGHT. The explanation is simplicity itself. (*A sudden impulse* .) Nothing but that. Put yourselves in my place. I come to London. I hear a vast deal of chatter about some articles in a paper called *The Echo* by some one calling himself 'Sampson Straight.' I also hear that nobody in London knows who Sampson Straight is. As I happen to *be* Sampson Straight, and as I have need of all possible personal prestige for the success of my purely patriotic mission, it occurs to me—in a flash!—to assert that I am the author of the famous articles…. Well, what more natural?

CULVER. What indeed?

STRAIGHT (*to* Tranto). And may I say that I'm the only genuine Sampson Straight in the United Kingdom, and that in my opinion it was a gross impertinence on the part of your contributor to steal my name? Why did you let him do it?

TRANTO (*beginning reflectively*). Now *I* hit on that name—not my contributor. It was when I was down in Cornwall. I caught sight of it in an old yellow newspaper in an old yellow hotel, and it struck me at once what a fine signature it would make at the bottom of a slashing article. By the way, have you ever been in the dock?

STRAIGHT. Dock?

TRANTO. I only ask because I seem to remember I saw your splendid name in a report of the local Assizes.

62

STRAIGHT. Assizes?

TRANTO. A, double s (*pause*) i-z-e-s.

STRAIGHT. I can afford to be perfectly open. I was—at one period of my career—in prison, but for a quite respectable crime. Bigamy—with extenuating circumstances.

MRS. CULVER (*greatly upset*). Dear, dear!

STRAIGHT. It might happen to any man.

CULVER (*looking at* Mrs. Culver). So it might.

STRAIGHT. Do you wish to detain me?

TRANTO. I simply haven't the heart to do it.

STRAIGHT. Then, ladies and gentlemen, I'll say good morning.

HILDEGARDE (*stopping* Straight *near the door as he departs with more bows*). Good-bye! (*She holds out her hand with a smile* !) And good luck!

STRAIGHT (*taking her hand*). Madam, I thank you. You evidently appreciate the fact that when one lives solely on one's wits, little mishaps are *bound* to occur from time to time, and that too much importance ought not to be attached to them. This is only my third slip, and I am fifty-five.

(*Exit, back* .)

MRS. CULVER (*to* Hildegarde, *gently surprised*). Darling, surely you need not have been quite so effusive!

HILDEGARDE. You see, I thought I owed him something, (*with meaning and effect*) as it was I who stole his name.

MRS. CULVER (*utterly puzzled for a moment; then, when she understands, rushing to* Hildegarde *and embracing her*). Oh! My wonderful girl!

JOHN (*feebly and still humiliated*). Stay me with flagons!

HILDEGARDE (*to her mother*). How nice you are about it, mamma!

MRS. CULVER. But I'm very proud, my pet. Of course I think you might have let me into the secret—

CULVER. None of us were let into the secret, Hermione—I mean until comparatively recent times. It was a matter between Hilda's conscience and her editor.

MRS. CULVER. Oh! I'm not complaining. I'm so relieved she didn't write those dreadful cookery articles.

HILDEGARDE. But do you mean to say you aren't frightfully shocked by my advanced politics, mamma?

MRS. CULVER. My child, how naïve you are, after all! A woman is never shocked, though of course at times it may suit her to pretend to be. Only men are capable of being shocked. As for your advanced politics, as you call them, can't you see that it doesn't matter what you write so long as you are admired by the best people. It isn't views that are disreputable, it's the persons that hold them.

CULVER. I hope that's why you so gracefully gave way over the baronetcy, my dear.

MRS. CULVER (*continuing to* Hildegarde). There's just one thing I should venture to suggest, and that is, that you cease at once to be a typist and employ one yourself instead. It's most essential that you should live up to your position. Oh! I'm very proud of you.

HILDEGARDE. I don't quite know what my position is. According to the latest news I'm dead. (*Challengingly to* Tranto.) Mr. Tranto, you're keeping rather quiet, nearly as quiet as John (John *changes his seat*), but don't you think you owe me some explanation? Not more than a quarter of an hour ago in this very room it was distinctly agreed between us that you would not kill Sampson Straight, and now you rush back in a sort of homicidal mania.

MRS. CULVER. Oh! I'd no idea Mr. Tranto had called already this morning!

HILDEGARDE. Yes. I told him all about everything, and we came to a definite understanding.

MRS. CULVER. Oh!

TRANTO. I'm only too anxious to explain. I killed Sampson for the most urgent of all possible reasons. The Government is thinking of giving him a baronetcy?

CULVER. Not *my* baronetcy?

TRANTO. Precisely.

MRS. CULVER. But this is the most terrible thing I ever heard of.

TRANTO. It is. I met one of my chaps in the street. He was coming here to see me. (*To* Culver.) Your answer was expected this morning. It didn't arrive. Evidently your notions about titles had got abroad, and the Government has decided to offer a title to Sampson Straight this afternoon if you refuse.

CULVER. But how delightfully stupid of the Government.

TRANTO. On the contrary it was a really brilliant idea. Sampson Straight is a great literary celebrity, and he'd look mighty well in the Honours List. Literature's always a good card to play for Honours. It makes people think that Cabinet Ministers are educated.

HILDEGARDE. But I've spent half my time in attacking the Government!

TRANTO. Do you suppose the Government doesn't know that? In creating you a baronet (*gazes at her*) it would gain two advantages—it would prove how broad-minded it is, and it would turn an enemy into a friend.

HILDEGARDE. But surely the silly Government would make some enquiries first!

CULVER. Hilda, do remember what your mother said, and try to live up to your position. This isn't the Government that makes enquiries. It's the Government that gets things done.

TRANTO. You perceive the extreme urgency of the crisis. I had to act instantly. I did act. I slew the fellow on the spot, and his obituary will be in my late extra. The danger was awful—greater even than I realised at the moment, because I didn't know till I got back here that there was a genuine and highly unscrupulous Sampson Straight floating about.

MRS. CULVER. Danger? What danger?

TRANTO. Danger of the Government falling, dear lady. You see, it's like this. Assuming that the Government offers a baronetcy to Sampson Straight, and the offer becomes public property, as it infallibly would, then there are three alternatives. Either the Government has singled out for honour a person who doesn't exist at all; or it has sought to turn a woman (*glancing at* Hilda) into a male creature; or it is holding up to public admiration an ex-convict. Choose which theory you like. In any case the exposure would mean the immediate ruin of any Government.

HILDEGARDE (*to* Tranto). I always thought you *wanted* the Government to fall.

CULVER. Good heavens, my gifted child! No enlightened and patriotic person wants the Government to fall. All enlightened and patriotic persons want the Government to be afraid of falling. There you have the whole of war politics in a nut-shell. If the British Government fell the effect on the Allied cause would be bad, and might be extremely bad. But that's not the real explanation. The real explanation is that no one wants the Government to fall because no one wants to step into the Government's shoes. However, thanks to Tranto's masterly presence of mind in afflicting Sampson with a disease that kills like prussic acid, the Government can no longer give Sampson a title, and the danger to the Government is therefore over.

TRANTO. Over! I wish it was! Supposing the Government doesn't happen to see my late extra in time! Supposing the offer of a baronetcy to Sampson Straight goes forth! The mischief will be done. Worst of all, supposing the only genuine Sampson Straight hears of it and accepts it! A baronetcy given to a bigamist! No Government could possibly survive the exposure.

MRS. CULVER. Not even if its survival was necessary to the success of the Allied cause?

CULVER (*gloomily, shaking his head*). My dear, Tranto is right. This great country has always insisted first of all, and before anything else whatever, on the unsullied purity of the domestic life of its public men. Let a baronetcy be given, or even offered, to a bigamist—and this great country would not hesitate for one second, not one second.

TRANTO. The danger still exists. And only one man in this world can avert it.

CULVER. You don't mean me, Tranto?

TRANTO. I understand that you have neither accepted nor refused the offer. You must accept it instantly. Instantly.

(*A silence* . John *begins to creep towards the door, back, and* Hildegarde *towards the door, L* .)

MRS. CULVER (*firmly*). John, where are you going?

JOHN. Anywhere.

MRS. CULVER. Have you still got that letter to Lord Woking in which your father accepts the title?

JOHN. Yes.

MRS. CULVER. Come here. Let me see it. (*She inspects the envelope of the letter and returns it to* John.) Yes, that's right. Now listen to me. Get a taxi at once and drive to Lord Woking's, and insist on seeing Lord Woking, and give him that letter with your own hand. Do you understand? (*Exit* Hildegarde, *L* .) The stamp will be wasted, but never mind. Fly!

JOHN. It's a damned shame. (Mrs. Culver *smiles calmly* .)

CULVER (*shaking* John's *flaccid hand*). So it is. But let us remember, my boy, that you and I are—are doing our bit. (*Pushes him violently towards the door* .) Get along. (*Exit* John, *back* .)

TRANTO (*looking round*). Where's Hildegarde?

MRS. CULVER. She went in there.

TRANTO. I must just speak to her.

(*Exit* Tranto, *L* .)

MRS. CULVER (*with a gesture towards the door, L*). There's something between those two.

CULVER. I doubt it. (*With a sigh* .)

MRS. CULVER. What do you mean—you doubt it?

CULVER. They're probably too close together for there to be anything between them.

MRS. CULVER (*shakes her head, smiling sceptically*). The new generation has no romance. (*In a new tone* .) Arthur, kiss me.

CULVER. I'm dashed if I do!

MRS. CULVER. Then I'll kiss you! (*She gives him a long kiss* .)

(*The lunch gong sounds during the embrace. Startled, they separate* .)

CULVER. Food!

MRS. CULVER (*with admiring enthusiasm*). You've behaved splendidly.

CULVER. Yes, that's what you always say when you've won and I—haven't. (*She kisses him again* .)

Enter the Parlourmaid, *back* .

PARLOURMAID. Miss Starkey is still waiting, sir.

CULVER. Inexorable creature! I won't—I will not—(*suddenly remembering that he has nothing to fear from* Miss Starkey; *gaily*). Yes, I'll see her. She must lunch with us. May she lunch with us, Hermione?

MRS. CULVER (*submissively*). Why, Arthur, *of course!* (*To* Parlourmaid.) Miss Starkey can have Master John's place. Some lunch must be kept warm for Master John. (*As the* Parlourmaid *is leaving* .) One moment—bring up some champagne, please.

PARLOURMAID. Yes, Madam.

(*Exit* Parlourmaid.)

CULVER. Come along, I'm hungry. (*Leading her towards the door. Then stopping* .) I say…. Oh well, never mind.

MRS. CULVER. But what?

CULVER. You're a staggering woman, that's all. (*Exit* Culver *and* Mrs. Culver, *back* .)

Enter Hildegarde *and* Tranto.

HILDEGARDE (*plaintively, as they enter*). I told you my nerves were all upset, and yet you ran off before I—before I—and now it's lunch time!

TRANTO (*facing her suddenly*). Hilda! I now give you my defence. (*He kisses her* .)

Enter Culver, *back, in time to interrupt the embrace* .

CULVER. Excuse me. My wife sent me to ask if you'd lunch, Tranto. I gather that you *will* .

CURTAIN.

Lightning Source UK Ltd.
Milton Keynes UK
UKHW010045170223
417092UK00003B/113